YOUNG CRUISERS

An Erotic Anthology

YOUNG CRUISERS

An Erotic Anthology

by

William Maltese

The Borgo Press
An Imprint of Wildside Press

MMVII

SECOND EDITION

contents

BEEN THERE, DONE THAT

Sloppy sounds could be sexy sounds. That these weren't, Ty Jackson's rubberized dick doggie-fucking a customer's ass, was a bit disconcerting to Ty who hoped he wasn't bored. A bored hustler was right up there with warm ice cream by way of desirability.

Ty couldn't blame Carr (with two r's) Milder ... or Milner .. or Maxner. Who the hell cared what his name was, since it was probably as play-baloney as they came? Ty always used his real name, but that was only because everyone assumed "Ty" had to be as phony as the next name.

Anyway, Carr wasn't all that bad to look at, especially considering he'd paid for the screw. He was probably in his early forties. He still had a full head of hair, gone only slightly salt-and-pepper ... more likely, salt and cinnamon, since the natural color seemed more brown than black. He had dark-colored eyes. Black, brown, maybe even dark blue. It had been just dark enough when he'd approached Ty that it had been impossible for Ty to tell. He had a regular nose. He had an attractively full-lipped mouth, probably really nice for sucking cock; Ty wasn't into mouths for kissing.

Carr's body wasn't all that shabby, either. Considering its age, it was in damned good shape. Ty had seen younger in far worse condition. Obviously, Carr spent time running, or playing tennis (maybe squash?), or working out in some local gym. It would have been nice to ask him, but customers, like Carr, didn't pay for conversation. Ty didn't usually give out information about himself, either, so why did Ty suddenly want an intelligent conversation, above and beyond fuck or suck, or that's my price, take it or leave it ... ?

"Ride my ass!" Carr said.

"Sure, stud, sure," Ty said. You didn't get a more meaningful conversation than that. "I'll drip my wick so deep you'll think it's lighting fire to your tonsils." Shit if Ty didn't sound like a porno movie!

Ty made the best of it. It was probably just a phase he was going through. It was probably just because he'd never really planned selling his cock forever and ever, amen. Then, again, it hadn't been forever. Not yet, anyway. All it had been was a year and a half. On the other hand, some of the graduates of the day's most ballyhooed educational institutions couldn't count as high as the number of tricks Ty had turned, in that very park, since he'd first taken money and pulled out his penis. Not too bad a score for a guy whose cock was only a little above average.

"Feel it? Feel it?" Ty asked.

"God, yes," Carr said. "Feels good."

Another reason Ty should be thankful was how Carr wasn't disappointed by how Ty's dick wasn't monster-size. A few of Ty's potential johns had gone so far as to ask for their money back. More than one of those had been given a black eye by Ty, in lieu of any refund. Damned size queens! Didn't anyone read Masters and Johnson, or whomever the hell had said a regular dick was only six inches? Ten inches wasn't normal. Eleven inches wasn't normal. Twelve inches wasn't a cock, it was a goddamned grotesque.

One guy, upon checking out Ty's six-and-a-half inches had said, "What saves you from seeing me walk is your bull-like balls." Ty had showed that prick what an average-sized prick could do. The shit, name of Roger (Ty still remembered his pseudo), had probably walked bull-legged for a good two days after Ty had finished with him. What's more, Ty had blasted so much cum from his impressive bull-like balls that he'd nearly ballooned the nippled tip of his rubber to bursting up Roger's none-too-tight ass.

"How's it feel, stud?" Ty asked Carr. It was voiced as Ty's genuine effort to come back to the here and now. Carr had paid his money, and he deserved Ty's undivided attention.

"Feels good, Ty. Mmmmmm."

"Want me to fist your dick, stud?" Ty didn't usually volunteer anything more than agreed upon in the original contract, but he felt Carr was being cheated. No matter if Carr figured he got the butt-fuck of his life, Ty just wasn't into it.

"No need," Carr said.

Poor bastard probably thought Ty would try to charge him extra. Ty knew some hustlers, in that very part of the park, who probably would have charged extra and probably did.

"Come on," Ty volunteered again. "Let's give your big dick the old heave-ho. On the house." Which sounded as if Ty were about to toss Carr's wanker onto some rooftop.

Ty took hold of Carr's cock without being given leave and, as usual, was a little jealous to hold a dick so obviously larger than his own. Damned, but Ty couldn't even get his hand around it. Did this shit know he could probably pull out his dick and have someone pay for it every time?

Ty palmed Carr's nuts with his other hand. Either Carr's scrotum had done some major scrunching, under the catalyst of

– 3 –

Cort Forbes

the pleasure Ty supplied, via his fuck of Carr's butt, or Carr's balls were far less impressive than his dick. Ty tried to remember just how Carr had looked when his pants had first come down.

Ty remembered Carr's fairly well-muscled and square pecs, Carr's fairly flat belly that still had a few muscled ridges left from better days gone by, an innie navel, a big cock, and an only slightly flabby ass. Ty couldn't remember how Carr's balls had hung in their scrotum, at that moment of their first unveiling.

"See how good that feels," Ty said, jammed his cock up Carr's ass, one more time, and simultaneously rode his hand along the full length of Carr's erection.

Doggie-style was a good fuck position. Carr on all fours. Ty on his knees and hunched over Carr from behind. Ty's cock up Carr's butt. Ty's hands on Carr's big cock and not-so-big balls.

"Jesus, yes!" Carr agreed. "Oh, yes ... oh, yes."

Give the guy a good time, Ty decided. Ty could be a pro's pro if he just concentrated. Ty had a year and a half of fucking to call on here to give Carr a ride the guy wouldn't soon forget. Pull out all the stops. Leave Carr talking about the experience for years to come.

"I'm going to come!" Carr said and shot to hell any of Ty's plans to extend the fuck anywhere beyond the moment at hand.

"Naw," Ty said, as if his words alone prevented it from happening. Ty really did want to show Carr a better time. "Let's make this last a bit longer, shall we?"

"Can't," Carr apologized.

As soon as Ty had fisted Carr's dick, Carr had known he was done for. He could get off with just cock up his ass, and the extra stimulation of Ty's fingers unexpectedly massaging not only Carr's cock but Carr's balls had simply been all she wrote.

Not that Carr was disappointed. A come was a come was a come. He would have liked as much hustler participation from the other hustlers he'd bought and paid for. Getting most of them to take a more adventuresome part was usually like pulling teeth. Hustlers would fuck Carr's mouth or ass, and that was usually it. Anyway, most all the hustlers Carr had ever found attractive had seldom contracted for more than that. Even Ty, before this pleasant exception, had been pretty straightforward, albeit pleasurably, it what he would and wouldn't do.

All of those were merely fleeting, disoriented thoughts, as Carr's orgasm took more and more hold and shook him literally senseless.

"Okay, then," Ty accepted the inevitable. He slid his dick to its hilt and left it there. He gave Carr's pulsing cock a hearty squeeze and collided one of Carr's erupting balls with the other within the palm of Ty's cupping hand. Then, all he did was hold on.

Ty accepted Carr's climax, but he didn't expect one for himself. He figured he'd let himself get too distracted during the lead-in. Maybe if he'd concentrated a bit more. Having figured too late to extend his fuck of Carr's butt, Ty might have done better to have tried coinciding Carr's orgasm with one of his own. Dual orgasms were hard to come by. Carr would certainly have remembered one of those.

Ty now merely waited for Carr to be over and done. The palm of Ty's fist, wrapping Carr's cock, actually felt the movement of Carr's cannonball cum as it exited Carr's balls, travelled the length of Carr's impressive erection, and squirted from the pouty cockmouth that cleaved Carr's circumcised cockhead like a hatchet blow cleaved a tree stump.

Therefore, it was with more than a good deal of surprise and

Cort Forbes

wonderment when a sudden series of anal shudders, around Ty's fully submerged cock, began the chain reaction, deep inside of Ty, that finally became more and more evident, to the point where Ty's handholds on Carr's dick and balls reflexively became more forceful.

The sudden additional pressure, more centred on his tender nuts than on Carr's more durable cock, actually enhanced Carr's pleasure. His moments of sublime ecstasy stretched into impossibly longer seconds.

"Fucking unbelievable!" Carr announced to no one in particular, although loud enough to be heard by two guys involved in oral sex several hundred yards away.

Had Carr really wanted to hear about something really unbelievable, though, he should have asked Ty for an example. Not that Ty could tell him, because Ty was too busy experiencing it to put it into words. Anyway, put it into any form of viable speech that was immediately decipherable as anything even vaguely human.

"Uggghhh, ughhhh, ahhhh, ahhhh, aggghhrrhu!" was just about all Ty could manage. Quite aside, of course, from his oceans and oceans of cum which suddenly were on the move, from original storage in his bull-like balls, along the total length of his average prick, and finally spouted from his cockmouth into the nippled tip of his rubber. So forceful were his explosions of soupy sperm that without the rubber to contain them, Carr would likely have been sure, as sunrise, that Ty's cum had jettisoned from Carr's asshole to Carr's throat, back-ass-wards.

All the while, Ty's pelvis delivered staccato little fuck strokes that barely ever had his dick out of Carr's asshole for more than a mere fraction of an inch at any one time. Carr's bunghole continued exerting pleasurable pressure along Ty's plugging inches,

– 6 –

even after Carr had officially stopped giving up the sperm which had filigreed Carr's belly, his chest, his neck, and even drooled his chin.

Ty's muscled asscheeks dimpled and relaxed, dimpled and relaxed, even when his cock no longer spewed cream. It was a reflexive tic, in aftermath, but no less pleasurable for Ty's inability to control it.

"Damn!" Ty managed finally, and it came out totally identifiable as words. Mere seconds before, it would have been garbled and guttural, as animalistic as any sounds before men were all that far removed from the primordial ooze.

Car could only agree with Ty's appraisal of the fuck. Not only would Carr immediately come away from this particular blast-off with thoughts that it was far and above most of his ejaculation, up to that point, but he would look upon it, years afterwards, as the butt fuck against which to judge all others.

Which didn't mean Ty and Carr didn't immediately revert to the usual uneasiness, embarrassment, even paranoia, that came after all the ecstasy-producing insulation, that had so completely kept them enraptured within a world of their own making, had completely faded away.

Ty's cock pulled free and brought Ty's cum-filled condom with it.

Ty removed his rubber while he was reared on his knees, his cock still stiff enough to provide a drawbridge that would have spanned the gap between Ty's belly and Carr's ass if only Car had kept his used and abused buttocks in place.

Carr, though, already scrambled to his feet, was already almost dressed before Ty decided whether to tie off his cum-bulged rubber, and carry it home with him, like a proper day-tripper, or simply toss the used condom into the bushes to one side.

Cort Forbes

Ty ran the flat of one hand up his muscle-welted belly and over his well-delineated pectorals. His hand's leading edge pushed a thin wake of sweat before it.

Ty still was stark naked, although standing, when Carr was almost disappeared up the park pathway.

Vaguely, Ty wished Carr had been so taken by the fuck that Carr would have insisted on taking Ty home with him.

Ty, from middle-class respectability gone horribly wrong only when his father had turned to drink, desperately wanted an eventual return to hearth and home. Instead, here he was, naked and inviting all comers, in a park known throughout the state as a place in which no respectable man would have been caught dead after nightfall.

"Fuck 'em!" Ty said to no one in particular, of no one in particular.

He ran his fingers through his hair, and his short black strands fell pretty much into their usual — if he could believe what he'd been told more than once — attractive tousle. With eyes so pale brown that people insisted they were gold, Ty slowly surveyed his immediate surroundings, disappointed no one seemed near at hand. He felt incredibly sexy, irresistibly attractive, and capable of, here and now, delivering the ultimate fuck to anyone lucky enough to come on up and ask for it.

His euphoria was short-lived. First, he seemed all too alone in a park he knew crawled with horny guys. Second, his cock, even less impressive soft than hard, had gone completely to almost virtual disappearance within the tangled pubic bush that sprouted Ty's lower belly.

He got dressed in black T-shirt, black jeans, black loafers. No underpants, no socks.

He was actually out of the park when he spotted the

Mercedes. At first, he ignored it and kept right on going. A few more steps, and he would have been around the corner and out of sight.

Something about the older man, so suddenly but tentatively out of the car, though, made Ty pause. Even then, Ty thought he merely saw another horny old man out to put a couple bills in the hands of some available hustler to pay for hustler cock fucked up old-man butt or mouth.

Except, Collin Drange turned right instead of left, and Ty was suddenly curious as to when and how the man would be made to see the error of his ways. Collin, at his age, wealthy or not, wasn't likely to find free sex where free sex, in the park, was offered. Free sex usually meant high-schoolers out for the thrill of a mutual grope or for membership in a mutual admiration society. Unless, Collin counted upon some kid needing a father-figure to fuck or be fucked by. How the hell old was the old coot, anyway? Certainly old enough to be Ty's father. That spotted easily enough, even from the distance.

Likely, someone had given Collin the wrong directions. Or, Collin had mistaken right from left. Or, Collin had parked in the wrong place, on the wrong side of the park.

Impulse decided Ty to play Good Samaritan. Certainly, it wasn't physical attraction. If Ty had a type, Collin definitely wasn't it. Collin, literally over the hill, no longer possessed even the slightest clue that he'd once been a stud for whom willing clients had paid hard cash for hard cock. Too much too good living, and too much dissoluteness, before and after his lover's death, had left Collin overripe, older than his none-too-young-at-any-rate years.

With a wad a cash, Collin might persuade some hustler to bare a bought cock for sex. Dollars might allow a hustler to overlook Collin's nose filigreed by veins. Lucre might make a hustler ignore Collin's cheeks too flush from overeating and overdrinking. Dinero might make a hustler blind to Collin's overhanging gut, to Collin's stick-like legs, all three of which had long since been deprived of muscle definition that had once turned the heads of envious body-builders at the beach.

The high-school kids who prowled that part of the park for which Collin was headed, would be downright rude about Collin's audacity in trying to join them. Ah, the cruelty of youth! Which hadn't really been truly recognized by Ty until he'd felt his own youth slowly begin its steady leak from him. If his youth wasn't completely faded, by a long shot, what had faded left him far removed from those narcissistic little shits who roamed the free side of the park and thought they'd remain young enough to do so forever.

Quickly and silently, from nights, sometimes all night, spent in this very kind of darkness, Ty headed for Collin who was slower, more tentative, and noisy enough, even on the grass, to announce his presence to anyone yards away. Not that anyone was all that interested.

"You look a little lost," Ty said and watched Collin actually leave the ground in surprise as to how Ty had managed to come up so close behind him, Collin completely unaware.

"Jesus, you scared the shit out of me," Collin said. Not an unpleasant voice but rough around the edges from years of indiscriminate drinking and experimentation, major and minor, with various drugs. "I was better at prowling in my younger days."

Close up, Ty was even less able to see the man as Collin had once been.

"You might try somewhere on the other side of that pathway," Ty said and motioned in the direction which would see Collin better served by what the park had to offer.

"The hustlers' meat rack, you mean?" Collin wasn't nearly as ignorant as Ty imagined. "I should be over there, while you're over here? Why is that, I wonder?"

"Anywhere is fine," Ty backpedaled. So much for doing a good deed. Ty had merely wanted to be kind, and it could well be that he, rather than some completely uncaring high-schooler, would be the one who ended up hurting this old fart's feelings.

Ty prepared his hasty retreat.

"Wait!" Collin insisted. He'd been lucky beyond belief in find-ing just what he wanted, so soon, but he could ruin it in a heart-beat.

Ty decided to quit while he was still ahead and kept right on going.

"Please!" Collin called after.

Ty stopped, turned back, came back, tried again.

"I obviously don't know what you're looking for, all right?" Ty said. "Guys with money usually prefer to buy their sex. It's less complicated for them that way."

"If I said I'm looking for something a bit more complicated?"

Good luck, buddy! is what Ty thought. What he said, though, was: "There's a lot of warm bodies, on either side of the park."

"If I said I'd already found the one warm body I wanted?"

Jesus, thought Ty, where to go from there?

"I'm flattered," Ty said, "but to be quite frank ..."

What? Collin was about as ugly as they came? Ty, who had always figured he could get an erection for a donut hole, just given a couple of minutes, doubted he'd ever get a boner for Collin, even if Ty's cock were fresh as a daisy and not already once drained by Carr's asshole?

"Look," Collin said, "I'm just looking for a little companion-ship. Someone with whom to enjoy a meal, my treat, and a lit-tle small talk."

"You want someone with whom to share a meal and small talk?" Collin might as well have tried to sell Ty the Brooklyn Bridge.

"That's all," Collin insisted.

"You're not here for sex?" You could fool some of the peo-ple all of the time, all of the people some of the time, but Ty did-n't buy any of Collin's no-sex bullshit.

"Look at the poor shape I'm in," Collin said. "Then, you tell me."

Damn, but Ty found Collin damned pathetic. Ty could offer to join the old fart for dinner. Ty was hungry. Over dinner, Ty could manage a bit of small talk. He'd just spent more of his time with Carr, than he should have, wishing there was someone he could just talk to, not having to service with his cock, one way or another, and here was that someone. On the other hand, Ty didn't really want to spend any more time than necessary with this poor sod.

"Come on," Ty said. So what if he was a softy!

"My car's that way," Collin reminded.

"We're not going to your car, are we?" Ty said.

"Where, then?"

"Somewhere a bit more private." Ty motioned toward the closest copse of trees.

"But ...?"

"Just two consenting adults, that's all." Even Ty wasn't sure why. Maybe the obvious challenge of sex with someone he found truly unattractive. If Ty could get off with Collin, he could get off with anyone or anything. If he couldn't, he could rationalize, to Collin and to himself, that he'd been too exhausted from blast-off up Carr's asshole.

Collin was suddenly afraid he might say something to talk Ty out of it. Ty's proposal, more than anything else ever could have, painfully brought home to Collin just how unlikely it really was for Ty to suggest what he'd suggested to the man Collin had become.

"It's all free on this side of the park," Ty reminded. "You'll even save the cost of feeding me."

Suddenly, Collin saw Ty less a sex object than someone out to lure him into deeper darkness in order to bang him over the head and steal his money. Except, this had gone down all wrong for a mugging. Ty had already been close enough to knock Collin unconscious, Collin completely unaware at the time, but Ty had only offered directions. Maybe Ty now saw an opportunity for a robbery he hadn't seen before.

Meanwhile, Ty fantasized a husky blond construction worker. He pictured the stud stark naked, except for hobnailed boots, utility belt, hard hat. The stud bent over a desk scattered with architectural designs. All Ty had to do was get his cock hard, and the fantasy stud's ass would be his.

"Give me your hand," Ty said to Collin. "Come on, give it over," he persisted.

Collin finally obliged.

"What do you suppose this is?" Ty asked and slowly, ever so slowly, placed Collin's hand over Ty's crotch. "It's not rock-solid cock, not quite yet, but it will be by the time we're among those trees."

Collin allowed himself a quick squeeze, convinced Ty's cock was swelling even farther. A boner because Ty found Collin a

– 13 –

turn-on? As believable as Collin might like to think that possible, he didn't think it was so. Knowing it wasn't so, though, did he reject Ty's offer of a perfectly respectable erection? Was Ty the most clever of hustlers? The kind who knew the best way to money was often not to ask for any money at all?

"Let's do this," Ty said and gave Collin the little pull that was all the momentum Collin really needed to commence a course of no return.

All Ty's plans remained short-range. First, succeed in a complete erection. Then, hopefully, get it off up Collin's mouth or butt. After that, get the hell out of there.

Ty believed he was merely prematurely out to sample, here and now, what would be his fate when his youth and beauty faded and he was reduced to servicing people like Collin. Depressing! So depressing that Ty's cock lost some of its hardness. Damned bad timing!

Ty reinforced his fantasy of the naked construction worker. It helped. If only Collin were even vaguely attractive, Ty would have been home free. Unfortunately ...

"How do you want it?" Ty asked, once he had Collin among the trees. "Up your mouth or up your ass?"

Collin wasn't fool enough to believe there were any other choices. Since he preferred not to be made even more vulnerable by his pants dropped ...

"What say, I see this dick I'm going to suck," Collin said.

No way did Ty drop his pants for this suck. Granted, he had to unbuckle, unbutton and unzip, in order to get his finally hardened prick out and his balls spilled into the open, but he re-buttoned and re-buckled to keep his pants anchored securely around his waist.

Collin was drawn to Ty's erection like an iron filing to a magnet. Collin's knees collapsed him to a kneeling position. He reached for Ty's cock and told hold. It wasn't all that big, but Collin had never been fond of choking on monster dick. Ty's cock was plenty big enough for what Collin and Ty had in mind for it.

"Jesus, a moment!" Ty insisted an jerked away so quickly that he almost left his hard cock detached and still in Collin's gripping fingers. "A rubber, man. My pecker needs a raincoat."

That Collin had forgotten the necessity for a rubber, in that day and age, proved to Collin it had been a helluva long time since he had been a member of the dating game. So long that he'd almost forgotten, too, those feelings so recently, and so mysteriously, resurrected to bring him here in the first place.

Ty was nervous by how close Collin seemed to have been to taking on Ty's unrubberized cock. Ty's hands actually shook as they draped his monkey with latex. At least this latest turn, to this truly macabre little adventure, hadn't drained any the stiffness from Ty's erection. Who was it who'd said fear was a powerful aphrodisiac?

"There," Ty said, his cock fully draped in latex. He aimed it in Collin's direction. "Much better, yes?"

Collin wasn't all that fond of rubbers. They made a dick look cataractous or, even worse, in some kind of a placenta, waiting to be born. A prophylactic's rubbery tip had a disconcerting way of tickling Collin's throat to distract him from the suck at hand. The same rubbery nipple, when filled with blasted cum, easily choked Collin like no naked cock had ever done. Besides which, rubberized dick tasted positively bland, while every naked dick had a flavor. The flavor of naked dick might tend toward funky, but it was never dull or uninteresting. Cum, too, had its own taste. Nothing like a mouthful of nutty spunk on the way down one's gullet.

Although Ty's cock didn't seem a leaker, no preseminal dew drops visible inside the cock-stretched latex, even pre-cum juices delivered deliciousness to be savored.

Frank and Collin had seldom used rubbers.

Frank and Collin, though, had been of another age. They'd met, courted, and bonded before AIDS. They'd been monogamous, for the most part, after AIDS.

Today was an entirely different ball game. God only knew where Ty's cock had been. Ty was such a good-looker, he probably couldn't even remember how many mouths or butts his dick had fucked. Each hole a potential breeder of the plague. All of which made Collin grateful that Ty had been so determined not to feed Collin naked cock. It made Collin confident that he dealt with a very conscientious young man.

Collin's hand returned to Ty's boner. The dick possessed a new, rubber-glove consistency. Nonetheless, it looked more and more inviting. It made Collin want to see more of Ty's obviously studly body, except asking Ty to strip now was, Collin knew, quite out of the question. It was a miracle Collin actually had been allowed to worship at Ty's phallic shrine at all. As much as Collin was reluctant to admit it, he suspected Ty was even more handsome than Collin had ever been. Nothing like the ravages of good living and old age to make a guy humble. There having been a time when Collin, like Ty, had only offered his cock for no more than fucking mouth or asshole. All that oceans and oceans under the proverbial bridge.

Collin tired of bemoaning what was no longer his. As Cher once sang: you couldn't turn back time. Anyway, something about turning back time. Damned if Collin really remembered.

Collin told himself to be content. He had a cock at his disposal, other than his own. A cock not too big, not too small, and fisted securely in his right hand. A cock ripe and ready for eating. A cock rock-solid.

Had Collin, in his prime, been able to get a boner for anyone or anything, anywhere? Frank, Collin's long-time lover, never exactly a picture of prime delectability.

Ty wished to hell Collin would get on with it. As long as the old boy was taking, Collin might well have decided Ty's cock really too small for sucking. Except, Collin still came across as a man desperately in need of any kind of cock to show him a good time. Trouble was, if Collin didn't get a move on, Ty couldn't guarantee the continued availability of his dick, at least his dick in erection. That Ty's cock was erect at all was only because he had a vivid imagination that, at least momentarily, metamorphosed Collin into someone handsome and studly. However, such conjurations couldn't be counted upon to last forever.

"Come on, stud, make a meal of my dick," Ty encouraged. "It's what you want. It's what I want. Not so hearty a meal, either, that you can't get it down in one hearty swallow. What do you say? Want to give the old one-gulp a try?"

Collin not only gave it a try, he succeeded with a skillful rapidity that gave Ty a genuine start. Because, there had once come a deciding moment, in Collin's relationship with his lover, that Collin had not only ended up sucking Frank's dick but had become damned good at sucking it, if only because he'd seen how a variety of sex had been necessary to keep his man. A constant menu of just Collin's cock up Frank's ass, and/or just Collin's cock up Frank's mouth, wouldn't have kept Frank landed for nearly as long as Collin had finally managed.

"Well, isn't that deep throat of yours genuinely nice," Ty said.

– 17 –

With his eyes closed, his cock locked up Collin's gullet, it was suddenly easier to imagine Collin, once the frog, now suddenly converted into Collin the studly construction worker. "Seems my cock was just made for your kind of sucking."

Collin was infinitely pleased with his mouthful. He genuinely liked its size. Frank's dick had been such an unwieldy big thing, it had kept Collin so constantly worried about choking on it that Collin had never really been able to enjoy a suck the way he would have liked.

Ty's cock fit Collin's mouth and throat nicely. Not even the cock's rubber-nippled condom had tickled all that much on the way down. Ty's dick had no difficult curves for Collin's mouth to manoeuvre, no thick-here, thin-there anomalies. It was consistently tubular, and Collin's throat was just the tube into which it fit, neither too loosely, nor too tightly.

Collin's nose, poked into the breach of Ty's open fly, pugged against Ty's lower belly, amid the hair that grew there. Collin enjoyed Ty's manly smells, even if he was deprived of Ty's manly tastes.

"Let's play merry-go-round horse, what do you say?" Ty suggested. It was easier to maintain his hard-on while it was stuffed up Collin's face.

Collins was suddenly just as anxious to proceed. It had been awhile since he'd sucked cock, and he wondered, after the easily achieved initial success of this first swallow, if cock-sucking wasn't something one never forget, like riding a bike.

Collin's hands locked to the backs of Ty's thighs, up where Ty's hard ass blossomed sexily to fill the seat of the stud's trousers.

Collin's face pulled up Ty's dick and left spit-drenched rubber behind it. Collin's lips found the groove formed by the flare of Ty's cockcorona. Collin gummed the groove, gave a massive suck, and swooped right back on down into the funky smells emanating from Ty's crotch.

"That's the way," Ty encouraged. "Now, you're talking." Not that Collin could manage to say anything even vaguely intelligible over the six inches of dick suddenly lodged against his vocal cords.

Collin thought: Oh, yeah, just like having learned to ride a bicycle. His head rode up to the head of Ty's cock, slid right back down again. Up, down ... up, down ... up, down, up. Like bicycle pedals went 'round and 'round and 'round.

Collin was so into the fuck, he played little games, like overtake his own spit. Collin's mouth released saliva while his lips were sucked to the very tip of Ty's erection. Collin watched his spit slide down Ty's rubberized dick. Before the wash actually met with and beaded within the cockhair bushed at the base of Ty's erection, Collin's falling face reclaimed it.

Ty's hands combed their way into Collin's hair. Ty was glad Collin still had hair. Collin without hair would have made it harder for Ty to maintain his fantasy of fucking the mouth of someone far younger and more handsome than Collin was.

"Let me show you just how I like it," Ty said. For free, he had complete say in the matter. Hopefully some equally handsome stud would be as prepared to take on Ty when the day arrived that Ty woke up unattractive, crusty, and old.

Ty's fingers tightened against Collin's scalp. His handholds moved Collin's sucking face into a cadence that matched the decided fucking motions Ty's hips took up in earnest.

"There now," Ty said. "Feels real nice. Real, real nice."

Yeah, Ty was more and more confident he'd pull this madness off. He was a magician, for Christ's sake! Hell, pulling rabbits out of a hat was nothing in comparison. Ty felt positively Christ-like.

Collin went with the flow. Not fearing strangulation made it all so much easier, so much more enjoyable. Yes, there actually was enjoyment to the mere slipping and sliding of Ty's cock, even Ty's rubberized cock, riding back and forth, back and forth, in and out, in and out, of Collin's face. So much pleasure, in fact, that Collin's dick responded by going rock-hard in Collin's pants. If not for Ty's possible objection to the distraction of Collin suddenly pulling out hard dick, Collin would have done so and beat off his cock in time to the fuck of Ty's cock up Collin's more-hungry-by-the-minute mouth.

Ty's cock found the hugging warmth, the pleasure-producing friction, the tugging and releasing vacuum up Collin's throat, some of what could be found in every mouth Ty's cock ever fucked. It was only a matter of degree that separated one cocksucker from the other. Unfortunately, a whole lot of that degree of separation was tied up in packaging. If only Collin came packaged even a bit better.

"Hmmm, hmmmmm, good," Ty said. There was some kind of soup commercial that had happy consumers in ecstasy over a mere spoonful. "We're definitely ... definitely ... on a roll here, buddy. We knew we'd get here all along, didn't we?" What bullshit! "Sure, we knew." Sure as hell, Collin hadn't known any such thing! "Yes, man, eat my stiffy dick. Eat it ... eat it ... oh, yeah, swallow and spit, swallow and spit ... swallow and spit my fuck-your-hungry-mouth wiener."

If miracles were about to send the latest of Ty's spermal loads pummelling into condom rubber, even stranger things were at work within Collin's balls. So marvellous were the sudden pleasurable sensations taking root in Collin's groin, without any manhandling of his erection, not even Collin believed what was happening was happening. Spontaneous orgasm was nothing he'd ever experienced, and he didn't even have a name for the definite build up of pressure exerted by his load of cum suddenly yearning to be free of his balls.

"Ahhhh, ahhhhh!" Collins tried to put sounds to the exquisite something he felt take more and more root inside him.

"Yes!" Ty was genuinely triumphant as the vibrations of Collin's sounds, unexpected as they were pleasurable, placed Ty on the very brink of orgasm. If only Collin had the intuitive expertise to ...

"I'm coming!" Collins literally screamed around Ty's face-fucking dick, although his words came out nowhere that intelligent. "I'm Jesus, fucking, coming!"

The additional sound effects, and the sensuous vibrations they provided the entire length of Ty's again fully submerged and locked into place dick, was all Ty needed.

"I'm coming, buddy," Ty said, even as the first slug of his spermal honey filled all the available space within the nipple of the rubber, without actually making the latex expand. "I'm actually ..." He fed another mess of his cum into the reservoir designed to contain it. "... coming ..." Another wad, comet-size, came free of his dick. " ... COMING!" he told whomever in the park was interested, which really only boiled down to Collin and him. Collin presently so consumed by the wonder of his own ejaculation, into the unsuspecting and certainly unprepared crotch of his undershorts, that he didn't even notice the ballooning of the condom down his throat.

Days later, Collin sat at the desk which had been Frank's desk.

He looked across the room of a house which had been

Cort Forbes

Frank's house, through French doors which had been Frank's French doors, to the pool which had been Frank's pool.

Young, virile, handsome Ty was poolside.

Any wonder Collin found himself, once again, reminiscing about Frank.

Frank who had been old when Collin first met him. Collin only twenty-two and hustling at the time. Oh, not hustling city streets. Not peddling his large cock and tight ass at some tacky meat rack, like the one in Boyland Park.

Collin a tour escort who had worked for a travel agency that had specialized in tours for older, richer, jaded gays. Collin conned older gay men, Frank included —as it were — into liking him enough to give him generous gratuities.

Frank had invited Collin for drinks on a day when Collin had spent the morning on a Thailand beach. Collin had been oh-so handsome in those days, made more so by having toasted golden brown in Asiatic sunshine. Not to mention the flattering brilliant orange of his swimming suit, color and suit design having focused attention on Collin's scalloped abdominals, on Collin's square pectorals, on Collin's well-developed arm and leg muscles. Then, there had been the way Collin's large cock and ample balls had so precariously filled the swimsuit crotch, swimsuit material stretched tight enough to reveal each and every vein that ran the impressive length of Collin's obviously erect cockshaft.

Frank had told Collin, in seeming passing, "I guess I'll try a world cruise next."

Collin had said, "I've never been on a cruise, nor 'round the world." He could spout double entendres with the best of them.

Collin had flashed white teeth, all his own in those days. People had always said he had an attractive smile. It had set off his square jawline, his cleft chin, and his dimples. It had made his sky-blue eyes twinkle as if he were genuinely amused.

Had Collin actually thought Frank would take him on that cruise. Certainly, he had called Frank for dinner, after the Thailand trip was over and done.

"I never really expected to see you again," Frank had later said. He'd underestimated Collin's persistence. He'd underestimated, or maybe not, how powerful an incentive a world cruise could be to a clever young hustler on the make.

On the cruise ship, fellow passengers had assumed Frank and Collin were father and son, or uncle and nephew. Frank eventually had come to resent the ease of those misconceptions, and he began to demand more and more sexual favors from his son/nephew in response. Collin, though, had come prepared to pay whatever the piper demanded. Nothing had ever been free for Collin in the world Collin had been born into and came from.

Only occasionally had Frank gotten downright maudlin about his ever-increasing old age. The best remedy Collin had found for it was taking hold of Frank's hand and placing it over Collin's crotch.

"Does that tell you anything but that, no matter what your age, you're still incredibly sexy?" Collin's had always said in accompaniment.

At that age, Collin had always had a hard-on.

Still remembering how it had been with Frank, Collin went to the chaise longue that couched Ty's near nakedness by the pool. Collin admired the young man's defined pectorals, virtually hairless except for silky black strands that haloed Ty's copper nipples Ty's abdominals couldn't have been any the more stereotypically washboarded. Ty's cock and balls were cupped within the crotch of Ty's royal-blue — irony not going so far as to have provided him with a brilliant orange — bikini.

"I love you," Collin said.

Ty pretended sleep.

Ty's navel was an attractive punctuation mark dead-center his stomach, and Collin bent to kiss it and let his tongue linger to sample the exotic flavors of virile young man, sweat, and a suntan lotion, the latter with decidedly coconut base. With the tip of his forefinger, Collin traced the faint outline of Ty's cock which was curled upon the impressive pillow provided by Ty's large scrotum.

Ty's cock was soft. Luckily, some soft things could got mighty hard. Some virile young men had a way of putting the hardness of their dicks forever at their beck and call.

"Marvellous," Collin said and patted Ty's flaccid dick. "Stay right there, and I'll be back shortly to say a far better hello."

Collin headed to the pool cabana, where he stripped and searched through a pile of potential swim wear. Luckily, there were no mirrors to reflect his nudity and tumble him into depression. In the end, he skipped a bathing suit and merely draped himself in a terry-cloth robe with two condom packets stuffed conveniently in a side pocket.

When Collin returned to the pool, Ty still faked sleep but his swimsuit was removed. On the flagstone, the crumpled material formed a surprisingly insignificant puddle of blue. The young man's cock was rock-hard, it's cockhead aimed toward Ty's navel, like a rocket aimed toward a crater on the moon. Not one of those monstrous rockets, of Russian origin when that country was in its now long-gone heyday, but one of the more modest, albeit nonetheless streamlined variety, say a French Exocet.

Ty's cock was already rubberized, because Ty remained

nervous by how easily Collin could have taken on Ty's naked cock when the two had first met in the park. Collin, though, was determined they would eventually shed such protection, but not shed safe sex, if after several months they both kept testing negative for AIDS and private-investigative reports verified Ty remained monogamously faithful.

Collin slid his robe off his shoulders and let it join Ty's swimsuit on one of the flagstones that bordered the pool. There was something very sensuous about how the slight breeze so intimately caressed Collin's most intimate body parts without being the least bit intrusive.

Collin planned little less subtlety than the breeze in his intended move on Ty's naked body. Not that Collin had any present intention of varying from the mutually agreed format for their sexual relations. Granted, somewhere up the line, Ty would have to come around to something a bit more adventuresome than just his cock up Collin's ass, or his cock up Collin's mouth, especially if Ty wanted to keep Collin's interest. That, though, was the future, Ty probably very happy to hear it. For quite a while yet, Collin would require no more than the amusements offered by the limited access allowed him.

Conveniently, the chaise longue on which Ty so sensuously sprawled had no arms. Just as conveniently, it was a substantially constructed piece of furniture. It had been selected with both characteristics in mind. There had been too much fucking done within the parameters of this property, too much fucking still to be done, to have furniture break under whatever the strain.

No guess as to whether or not his cock would, this time around, be up Collin's asshole or mouth, Ty had left his rubberized cock unbuttered. Far easier for Collin to soak it down with lubricant for a fuck than to find it soupy with industrial goo if Collin had sucking on his mind. Condom-company lubricant was edible but definitely an acquired taste that Collin, only recently introduced to the necessities of condom use, hadn't yet acquired.

Collin sat sidesaddle on the same chaise longue as Ty's passive body. He reached for the bottle of suntan lotion on the nearby low-standing table, and he unscrewed the cap. He tilted the open end of the bottle directly over Ty's dick and gave the dark-brown plastic container a gentle squeeze. Pleasantly smelling coconut-based liquid ran like clear treacle to cover the belly of Ty's stiff dick.

It didn't take much lubricant, because there wasn't all that much of Ty's dick. Even miserly squirted, there ended up more than enough oil to add a bit of glisten to Ty's balls. Ty's black pubic hair, on his scrotum and on his crotch, soon glistened in the same sunlight that so attractively illuminated the rest of the young stud's highly tanned body.

"Lovely, lovely cock," Collin said and fisted Ty's stiff meat to better smear its entire length and girth with lotion.

Ty shifted slightly, and Collin remained amused by Ty's little game of being molested while he slept. If the game was thrown just a tad off-kilter by Ty's cock not only hard but pre-rubberized — if not in preparation for receiving Collin's mouth or ass, then for what? — fantasy was whatever you wanted to make it.

"Lovely dick that I'm sure won't mind a workout up my butt while its sleeping and handsome owner has nothing better to do with it," Collin said.

When Collin's asshole came after Ty's cock, it was by Collin facing up Collin's body, and facing the head of the chaise longue, then straddling both Ty and the chaise longue, like a horseman having mounted a stallion and saddle. No way a genuinely sleeping Ty would have maintained even the deepest sleep with all the unsightly curvature of Collin's fleshy ass suddenly weighing down and overspilling Ty's lap.

When Collin lifted his ass and put it down again, it still wasn't to force-feed Ty's cock to it. It was more carefully to fit Collin's assbuns down and over the length of Ty's cock, like a hot-dog bun, down and over a steam-wet wiener.

Collin thoroughly enjoyed the young man's thick black eyelashes, on still-closed eyelids. Ty's lashes resembled feather fans against the upper edges of Ty's cheekbones.

Collin slid the slice of his ass forward and back, forward and back, along the length of Ty's greased pecker, like a massive train car not quite certain whether or not to risk the seeming precariousness of only a lone monorail.

Ty turned his face slightly sideways, as if somehow vaguely disturbed in his continuing sleep.

"Time for some real fun and games," Collin said.

Sliding one more time so that his pucker overhung Ty's balls, Collin lifted his ass as high as necessary to reach underneath and manhandle Ty's dick to a vertical stance beneath Ty's butthole.

"Down elevator," Collin said.

With a big smile, he lowered his ass until Ty's condom nipple tickled the entrance to Collin's asshole. Collin sat a bit more, and the nipple, never so rigid it could successfully boss open Collin's sphincter on its own, mashed between Collin's pucker and the pressing head of Ty's dick.

"Last stop before the basement," Collin said and waited just long enough to deliver the jiggle of his ass that persuaded him how perfectly Ty's cock was aligned to the mouth of Collin's butt.

Cort Forbes

With only a bit more drop, Collin's asshole opened its pucker over Ty's cockhead and gobbled Ty's erection all of the way to Ty's cockballs. Collin felt the wiriness of Ty's lotion-slicked pubic hair press intricate designs into Collin's landed buttflesh.

"Mmmmm, yes," Collin said, appreciatively. A few days before, the very first slide of Collin's asshole over Ty's cock had been the scariest. Not because Ty's six-and-a-half inches were nearly impressive enough to threaten even a virgin asshole with splitting, but because Collin had feared all his years of taking on Frank's overly large erection had made Collin's anus less than cozy accommodations for anything smaller. For that matter, what with the constipation of old age, Collin had shat a sewer full of turds bigger than Ty's dick.

However, whether Collin's asshole had repaired itself, like some lizards tails could repair themselves after having been severed, or whether Frank's big dick hadn't done nearly the damage Collin had imagined, Ty's cock fit as comfortably up Collin's butt as it fit in Collin's mouth. Not so filling that Collin felt any immediate urge to shit himself rid of it, but not so loose that Collin doubted he had six-and-a-half inches of something heavenly jabbed up his butt.

"Mmmmm," Ty mumbled in his supposed slumber. If anyone was delighted by how Collin's flabby ass provided a sensible fit, it was Ty who would have been hard-pressed, fantasies or not, to get his rocks off in anything looser.

"Surprising how we seem so made for each other," Collin said as much to himself as to Ty. "Yin and yang. Nut and bolt. Fred and Ginger. Dorothy and Toto. Your cock and my asshole."

His hands rested on either side of Ty's neck. His fingers slid down and over the young man's chest to where Ty's nipples pleasantly punctuated Ty's impressively delineated pectoral folds. Collin pinched the nubby centers of Ty's nipples and gave them simultaneous tugs, as if he expected to pull forth, like a tape measure from its container, the means by which to better guide the horse Collin had chosen to ride. That Ty's nipples went hard beneath the abuse was the trigger mechanism that spurred Collin onward to the next phase of his ride.

"Up greased pole," Collin said, and his ass rode Ty's dork all of the way to where Collin's sphincter found the groove where Ty's cockhead flared into existence. "Down greased pole," Collin said and reversed direction.

Collin was delighted by how well his body, mouth and ass, adapted to Ty's adequate, if not stupendous appendage. Everything seemed to fit almost too perfectly. Of course, Ty might not find the fit as much to his liking when faced with his eventual taking of Collin's far bigger cock into Ty's mouth and ass, but such differences were of less concern than if Collin had been dissatisfied by the way things presently stood. Not that Collin hadn't been prepared for far less.

"Let's play bang Collin's prostate," Collin said.

He angled his next up-and-down bounces so his prostate got just the massage the doctor ordered. In his younger days, such a workout of his prostate would have caused leakage of preseminal juice from Collin's pecker, but that artesian sexual well, always a source of pleasure to Frank whose cock never produced similar oozings, had long ago gone dry.

"Meanwhile, what do you think of old Collin's big dick?" Collin said and noted with excitement what was going hard between his legs. "Still a bit of starch left in the old battering-ram, wouldn't you say?"

Ty thought it way too much starch. He would have much

preferred Collin's erectile abilities more commensurate with what was more stereotypically expected from a man of Collin's obviously advanced age and deteriorated physical condition. Or, at least Collin's cock might have been a little more Ty's size than nearly half again as long and half again as bulky.

"Just look at the new life your cock puts into mine," Collin said. For a good year after Frank died, Collin thought himself impotent. As if Frank, begrudging whatever enjoyment Collin might discover without him, had taken all Collin's boners into the grave with him. "Feels mighty good stroking this big dick of mine while your hard-on provides one mighty fine ride for my asshole."

Collin thought about soaking his dick with oily suntan lotion but decided, at least for the moment, to beat his dick just as it was. He liked the firmness of his grip around the circumference of his dry meat. He liked the heat of friction from hearty masturbatory strokes of his unlubricated hand over his unlubricated erection.

"Quite frankly, or should I say, Quite Frankly ..." Collin smiled at his little pun and hoped the ghost of Frank wouldn't soon be back to haunt him, memories of Collin's dead lover already too frequently recalled. "... I feel positively reborn, Ty, my boy. And, you are young enough literally to be my boy, do you know that? Probably not once, not twice, but even three times over, mere youngster that you so obviously are."

Maybe there was something to the once-thought old wives' tale, told by old white slavers, of how a naked young slave, placed beneath the covers of the Old Massah's bed, could absorb whatever weariness the plantation owner had been forced to endure during the course of any given day.

Or, Collin might have commented upon how, if Ty would just open his eyes, he could view the illusion of Ty's cock so big and so long that it had thrust all of the way through Collin's ass and out the other side into the fist with which Collin now pumped away.

Collin, though, didn't say anything he intuitively sensed Ty might misinterpret as Collin somehow preferring a bigger cock up Collin's ass. Men like Ty, with small to middling dicks, never cared to believe that monster-dicked men could find it extreme-ly difficult to find willing mouths or assholes to take on their over-abundant phallic offerings. There weren't all that many size queens in the world, no matter how often it sometimes seemed they had all gathered at one and the same time, at one and the same place.

If miracles of Biblical proportions could occur from some-thing as small as a mustard seed, equally marvellous things could and did arise from a mere six-and-a-half inches of steely hard meat.

So, Collins kept most of such ongoing thoughts to himself and concentrated mainly on coordinating his pinching and tug-ging of Ty's right nipple, his beating his own meat, and his bouncing his ass over Ty's erection.

"Going to give me some cream, this time around, my boy?" Collin finally did ask, surprised by how quickly his fucked butt and hand-whipped dick worked together to conjure the upsurge of pleasure loose within him. Equally surprising was how often Ty managed to match Collin come for come. Granted, Collin had been able to do the same trick for Frank, but Frank had been as quick to express his amazement.

Collin really got into the bounce of his ass over Ty's cock, and into the bounce of his fist over his hand-fisted erection. How many men his age could boast their crotches sprouting erections anywhere nearly as steely as his, or claim nearly as sexy a hard cock as Ty's rammed up their aging rear ends?

"Oh, stud ... stud ... stud-cock up my ass ... stud," Collin said and gave Ty's nipple another hearty twist and tug. Nipple twisting and tugging was something that always had helped Collin get hot and bothered for Frank, and he hoped Ty would remember just how good it felt so, one day soon, Ty could perform the same service over Collin's burgeoning nipples. None of that needed now, Collin quite excited enough, thank you very much.

Ty had already decided that the time Collin spent abusing Ty's nipple was time well-spent. Something about the pain of almost having the nub of his nipple twisted free of its anchorage merely supplemented Ty's pleasure as derived from Ty's cock up Collin's ass, rather than detracted from it. So much so that Ty could finally admit to the definite possibility of his joining Collin in orgasm, one more time. Although, he still wasn't sure he could summon his own ejaculations as much on cue as Collin and he would have liked him to.

"Ooohhhhh, yesssss," Collin said. His ass slid up, his ass slid down. "Taking me to the brink, stud. Your cock doing that ... doing ... Jesus, doing ... that."

Collin's hand jerked his dick's loose outer cockskin up his solid inner cockcore. His hand returned the same loose skin on a downward course that collided the heel of Collin's fist with the bulge of Collin's compact scrotum. The pouty mouth of Collin's dick actually went damp in expectation of cum soon to follow.

Knowing Collin was close to orgasm, Ty angled Ty's butt-fucking dick for maximum masturbation within Collin's anal tubing. If Ty's cock seemed to fit, no matter whichever way it went in and out of Collin's butt, there were ways it felt just a tad better, and Ty worked hard to find them. Work, after all, was how he saw this. A job to be done and done well, if Ty expected to glean the

rewards he knew were his for the taking. If only he could summon up all the necessary tricks he'd learned of the trade, during
his year and a half of peddling his cock to paying customers who
cruised the meat rack in Boyland Park.

"I got buckets-full of cream just for you," Collin said.

His nuts were suddenly chock full of it. Surprisingly, they
weren't stretched enough, by the added weight of his sperm, to
touch down, as they had at the beginning of the fuck, atop Ty's
rippled belly. Instead, Collin's scrotum had lovingly hoisted his
testicles near the base of Collin's dick and kept them there. If
Collin's scrotum and balls didn't provide quite as compact a
package as they had in Collin's prime, nor had produced nearly
as much pearly cum as in the good old days, nevertheless ...

"I'm going to shoot !" Collin told Ty, just in case the kid needed just a bit more incentive to squirt Ty's cum up Collin's ass at
one and the same time. "I'm going to ... squirt ... hard ... and ...
Jesus, oh, Jesus ... here it comes ... comes ... comes!"

Right on cue, Ty's cock, again lost completely up Collin's
ass, the latter having sat totally down over Ty's entire dick the
moment Collin's hand-gripped erection started blasting, decided
to oblige and join in the fun and games.

Collin's cum erupted in gobs that didn't become airborne
nearly as high and as wide, nor travel nearly as far, as the cum
of his earlier years. More than once, in just such a straddle position, Collin's young dick had blasted soupy comets over Frank's
belly, Frank's chest, Frank's neck, and Frank's chin, to touch
down right atop the hole Frank's oh-that's-mighty-fine mouth had
formed when the man had really been in the deep throes of passion. These days, the majority of Collin's discharge merely over-
flowed the mouth of his cock, like immensely viscous volcanic
magma over the lip of a crater. No matter, in that it wasn't so

much how high-flying Collin's sperm could manage, as it was the intensity of the ecstasy that accompanied whatever the bubbling.

"Ugh! Ugh! Ughhhhgh!" Collin machine-gunned verbal response to each and every jolt of pleasure that kept perfect tempo with the pulses that oozed more and more of his creamy cum from his erection.

Ty's cum flooded condom nipple and made the small latex teat swell larger, ever larger, with each new hearty bullet fired from Ty's cock to join with the others that already threatened the prophylactic with bursting.

"Yes!" Collin reacted to his sudden realization that his pleasure was enhanced by Ty's suddenly throbbing cock and by Ty's suddenly cum-ballooned rubber shoved deep up Collin's ass. "Cum, kid ... Jesus ... kid ... cum ... kid ... up ... your daddy's ... hugging ... hugging ... tight old ass!"

Ty pressed his head back into the support offered by that part of the chaise-longue cushion upon which it laid. His Adam's apple bobbed like a cork in a bottle, his gasps surprisingly silent as they escaped through the partial opening between his sensuously full lips. Behind his closed lips, his gold-colored eyes twitched, as if in REM sleep. A trickle of sweat-saturated suntan oil cascaded the serrated length of his pectoral cleavage and spilled out upon the ridged plains of his passion-bulged abdominals.

All Collin's noticeable sexual movement culminated in one final cataclysmic shudder that left the man as exhausted as any cowboy who had ridden the meanest bronco to complete submission.

Despite all of his determination not to let go just how good his ride had been, fearful as he was that he'd lose some of his advantage over Ty if Ty ever discovered just how lucky Collin knew himself to be in having found Ty without hardly trying, Collin said: "Jesus, fucking, Christ, that was good!"

After which, Ty sleepily opened his gold, gone-bedroom eyes and flashed Collin a wide, almost merry grin.

"Have I told you lately that I love you?" Ty asked.

"Do you? Love me?"

"Lots and lots."

It was a boldface lie. Ty knew it. Collin knew it. But, that it was a lie really didn't matter at all.

BLACK AND BLUE

"Blue!" I'm surprised to see him.

"Blue?" he doesn't recognize the name I've given him.

I try to explain: "That first time I saw you..." I'm embarrassed. "... fucking, in Boyland Park ... I mean ..."

"Mmmmmmm?" His way of encouragement.

"The shadows and the moonlight made everything look blue. You know how they sometimes do."

"Made me look blue?"

"Yeah."

"Speaking of blue..." Apparently, my explanation is satisfactory. "... and black," he says. "I understand those two colors, if black can really be considered a color, are the reasons we've not seen your studly body lately."

I'm confused, but only momentarily. "Right," I admit. "Black and blue. Like my ass, you mean?"

"Yeah, like your ass. I thought I'd come by and take a look."

I blush. I still do that, although not as much as I used to. I still get embarrassed by blushing, too. Which still makes me blush all the more.

"I like it when you blush," he says. Which turns me an even darker shade of red. Thank God, my work-on-it-everyday tan partially mutes the effect.

"I don't like it." No truer words I'd ever spoken.

"Wait until you're so jaded you can't blush no matter how

hard you try," Blue says. "Then, tell me you don't wish you had the knack back again."

"Yeah, I'll get back to you."

"Until then, about your paddle-bruised ass. You want to drop your drawers, here in the hall, and let me take a look? Or, shall we go inside your apartment?"

"Hey ..." and I almost call him Blue again, because I don't really know his name, never have, although I've known him most of eight months. "... my mom ..."

"Isn't due back until nine," he breaks in. "She's got that new job at Bakeman's Eatery, or have you forgotten?"

My how'd-you-know expression makes him laughs. I'm a sucker for Blue's laugh. Not to mention for his blue-black hair, his green eyes, his dimples, his cleft chin, his muscled body, his tight ass, and his, last but not least, experienced and impressively large cock.

"I make it a point to keep track of people I like," he says. "I like to come visiting when they feel poorly. Whether they've a bad case of poison oak, a black-and-blue ass, or whatever else, had from getting naked in the park."

I step back to let him on through. I'm flattered, and not just a little, that he's stopped by. Our relationship has always been friendly, even more than friendly if you want to take into account how I chose him to break in my cherry ass. Or, rather, how he picked himself; I've never been all that sure, to this day.

"The place is a dump," I apologize.

"Naw," he disagrees. "It's nice. What's more, you've got a momma who worries about you and actually comes home at night. You don't know how good you've got it, kid."

I shut the door to the hallway and hope to God none of my nosy neighbours picked up on any of our conversation. Mrs.

Parkwater, two doors down, is particularly curious, but, luckily, stone deaf, in the bargain. Mr. and Mrs. Talbot should be at work. Mrs. Simpton, across the hall, should be ...

"So, you going to let me check out your ass, or what?" he interrupts my flustered train of thought.

"Thanks for stopping by, but my ass is a lot better. Really." The mere thought of dropping my pants for Blue, no matter how innocent and well-intentioned, gets me excited. Within my pants, my cock gives a visible jerk toward erection, and I blush some more.

"It's not as if I haven't seen your ass before, kid. You know?" He raises his left eyebrow the way I've tried to do but never can. He has this playful, shit-ass grin that only makes him more attractive. "Or, maybe, that other occasion was so unremark-able you've forgotten."

Fat chance of that kind of memory loss, this side of senility.

I unbuckle my pants. Not to do otherwise insinuates I give sexual significance to what's happening. Except, what does my still-engorging cock tell him?

"Come on, kid, this is Blue, here." He's picked up on my nickname for him as easily as he's picked up on all those other names his paying customers provide him nightly, in Boyland Park, in answer to his, "Who would you like me to be tonight, buddy?" He plops sensuously into a nearby chair, hooks one knee over the chair arm, and says, "You used to watch me all the time, that hard dick of yours pulled out on a clockwork basis, giving me extra incentive to fuck any old codger's ass."

Have I ever seen Blue fuck old-codger ass? Oh, he's fucked plenty of ass, no doubt about that. And I've seen him do the deed on innumerable occasions. But Blue has his pick of the paying customers who frequent the park, and he fucks studs so good-looking they could get fucked for free, any day of the year, just on the other side of the park, if they really wanted.

"You need a little help there?" Blue volunteers. "Button stuck?"

"Don't get any ideas that my boner has anything to do with you," I say. Then, I drop my pants.

"Of course it doesn't have anything to do with me," he says. "Not any more than this woody in my pants has anything remotely to do with you."

My glance goes automatically to his crotch, and his hand is already cupped there, his fingers pressing an additional emphasis to the tenting his erection makes in the denim. There's so little room for his cock, between his muscled thigh, and the tight cloth of his trousers, I can see the point where his cockhead stops and his cockshaft begins.

I pretend I'm not impressed, nor in the least turned on. "You could get hard for a hole in a watermelon," I tell him.

"Don't knock fucking fruit," he says and grins from ear to ear. "Why, when I was living on the farm... But, we're not here to discuss my sexual awakenings, are we?"

Actually, I wish we were. I know so little about him. Our relationship consists, up until this point, of sexually charged meetings in the park. Sexually charged for me, anyway, ever since I first watched him fuck. More sexually charged when I finally got around, on Blue's insistence, to jacking off while I watched him fuck. Genuinely going over the top, sexually, when I let him fuck my cherry ass. Since he initiated me into the wonders of gay sex, and since I've sampled some of the additional wares the park has to offer, above and beyond the obvious physical attributes of Blue, whom I suspect fucked my ass for free primarily because it was cherry at the time, we mainly see each other only in passing.

"Kind of hard to see much of your ass with your shorts still on," he tells me.

"What the fuck!" I decide. To my embarrassment and dismay, my shorts momentarily tangle on the stiffness of my now fully burgeoned joint.

"Well worth the wait," Blue says. "Now, shuffle on over so I can get a better look."

In for a dollar, in for a dime, or in for a penny, in for a pound, or whatever the appropriate goddamned adage ... metaphor ... or whatever.

"Now, don't you genuinely entice me with that big juicy cock of yours," he says when I'm in front of him. My cock never seems so big, or so stiff, or so impressive, as when Blue is near. As for the juicy part, my cock leaks clear, sticky lubricant, non-stop whenever sex with anyone is fantasized.

His hands are firm on my hips as he turns me butt-toward-him. He whistles; I could never do that without sounding like a loose fart.

"Your ass still looks downright cherry, you know that, kid?" He's probably never going to give me a higher compliment. "You aren't some kind of renewable virgin, are you, like some chick who regrows her hymen after each fuck?"

"I should be so lucky!" I very well know Blue's preference for cherry ass.

"Well, virgin ass definitely does have a lot to recommend it," he says, "but I don't see any indications, from my present view-point, that you should have any complaints with what you've got here. Except, of course, for this..." He touches one of my bruis-es. "...and this, and this, and this," he moves right along. I know the bruises are there, not only because I experience the discomfort from them, but because I've felt varying discomfort from them all week long; besides which, I've checked them out with my butt backed up almost against my bedroom mirror. "Still hurt, do they, kid?"

"Not much."

"But hurt getting them, yes?"

"Yes?"

"The black man really able to lay on the paddle, yes?"

"Yes?"

"But the handcuffs are just for show, right? They don't really lock. You can slip them off at any time?"

"That's how it goes."

"But you didn't slip them off?"

"I wanted the experience."

"And?"

"Now I've had it, I don't want it again."

"Not even when the black man pays so damned well?"

"Not even when."

"You wouldn't need to turn over several tricks an evening if you just let the black stud paddle and fuck your ass once every other week."

I enjoy turning tricks. The novelty of sex with men hasn't nearly worn off. The money is purely extra, especially now that my old man, less dead-beat than he's been for seventeen years, is back in my life and trying to buy my forgiveness; mom isn't so easily bribed and still refuses to see him.

"Yeah, well one look at my ass should tell you why I'm passing on any seconds," I tell him.

"When you were little," Blue says, "did your mother ever kiss your ouches and make them go away?"

He kisses my bruises, one after the other. It makes the pain seem less by temporarily concealing it beneath the exquisite pleasure of his lips, light as butterfly wings, against my rear end.

As much as I enjoy , I've got this gnawing, deep inside, that makes this less pleasurable than it should be.

"Why is it you're really here, Blue?" Whether he's John, or Peter, or Bill, or James, he'll always be Blue to me.

"I want to kiss your sweet ass a few times." After his pursed his lips, once again, touch down, on each of my bruises, he says, "A guy can't come around to check out his favorite ass of all time?"

"Flattery will ..." I'm going to say, "get you nowhere", but that would be a lie. I'm a sucker for just about everything Blue says, does, or is.

"You've been a little stingy, as far as your body-beautiful lately," he accuses. "Where I used to see you nightly, you don't come around all that often, if ever, anymore. I miss you, standing there, jacking off that big prick of yours while I screw some guy's asshole. Guess you're too busy doing the fucking, these days, to watch me do it? Not that I can blame you, but I miss the extra something I always got, seeing you standing there, cock in hand, jism-smeared fingers, while I blasted my wad up some guy's asshole."

Yeah, flattery will get Blue a helluva lot, and he knows it.

"I have dreams about this ass of yours, you know that?" he says. "Wet dreams no less. They have me creaming my sheets like some kid whose nuts have just dropped and who's just discovering what this thing called sex is all about."

His hands run from my hips to the back of my knees. He lies one cheek against an asscheeks. His breath is warm and sexy on my butt.

"Sometimes, when I screw some guy, I imagine it isn't his

butt I'm screwing but yours. You think any of that accounts for my grabbing the first excuse to come around and see about having seconds with this ass of yours?"

"You're kidding, right?" I don't want him to be kidding, but I know he is, and I wonder why.

I do an about-face that makes his cheek slide along my hip until my erect cock actually whacks him a good one across the side of his face. His cheek gets splattered with preseminal goo.

He doesn't pull away. He buries his juice-damp face into my crotch and sucks up my nuts, one large testicle at a time.

"Jesus, Blue!" My hands comb his thick, short-cropped hair. His blue-black strands are sensuous as silk. Inside his warm and wet mouth, my nuts collide and spill a surprisingly pleasurable ache into the pit of my belly. "Jesus, Blue!" I repeat, like a goddamned Polly-want-a-cracker parrot.

"What say you let me fuck your ass again?" he says when he comes up for air.

"My ass is no longer cherry," I remind him. "Your cock has seen to that, as well as have a few other cocks since yours."

"It looks surprisingly cherry," he says and cocks his head to attempt a better view of my ass now faced away from him. His hands slide around my hips and cup my buttocks. "Feels like cherry ass, too."

"You and I know your cock hasn't been the only one in it, though, don't we?" Why in the hell am I talking him out of it? I'd like nothing better than to be fucked, one more time, by his big and sexy cock. All the fucks that came after his weren't nearly as good. Maybe that's because his was the first. Maybe I'm reluctant to be won over, this time, because I don't want less enjoyable seconds from him that'll dilute my memories of our first time.

"Not all that many cocks after mine, though, the way I hear it." He looks up, silly-ass grin on this face, green eyes sexy as hell. "Maybe a grand total of five, including Mr. Black who first used his paddle in foreplay."

Blue's handsome face, so close to my erect cock, literally takes my breath away.

"You've got more of a reputation, these days, as a stud on the delivering end of a penis," he says and licks the base of my erection. "Some of my regulars are beginning to get the notion of giving your cock a try."

"You let me know which ones, and I'll tell them to get lost!" I mean it, too. Although, I'm disappointed his reason for coming is to complain of possible future business loss.

"Jesus, kid!" He bows his forehead against the belly of my stiff dick. He speaks to my balls, "You think I'm here to warn you away from my paying customers. Naw!"

How patronizing I must sound! Nonetheless, jerk that I am, I merely voice what I think. What other explanation? Blue here, because he has this "thing" for my ass, even if my ass is no longer virgin? I should be so fucking lucky!

"I'm glad you came." I try not to hem and haw and make things worse. "And I'm genuinely flattered, because something tells me you didn't make any similar sympathy call on the kid who got beat up by that skinhead, or on the guy who tripped on that tree root and broke his leg, or on the last sucker who let himself be handcuffed by that black man, leaned over the stub of that tree, and had his ass paddled black and blue before fucking?"

Blue looks up the length of my cock. I'm glad that he smiles. I like his being there, and I don't really care why or what brings him.

"Let's see ... did I visit any of those guys?" His nose rubs the belly of my cock in an kind of Eskimo kiss.

"I already know the answer, Blue." His blue-black hair is so expertly cut that, no matter how much it's manhandled or wind-blown, its silky strands always feather back into a not-too-perfect but just-right neatness.

"None of those guys have the dream-ass you do," he excuses.

He leans back into the easy chair. His face is no longer at my crotch, and I miss it being there. I miss the possibilities for his mouth opening to swallow all of my leaky erection to its thick roots. It's not the first time, in Blue's presence, I've imagined unsafe sex with someone whose unknown history could well make him a walking time bomb.

"First off," he says, "when I say some of my customers are tempted, and that's no lie, that doesn't mean they're preparing to leave me, like rats deserting a sinking ship." The flat of his hand raises and keeps me from interrupting. "After all, the majority of my regulars pay me not just because I've a big dick, and I'm damned good putting it to the kind of work a big dick like mine is best used for, but because they've bought the whole well-hung, tall, dark and handsome, been-around-the-block package. We queers have our own specific sexual likes and dislikes, just like everybody else. The johns who pay you want someone decidedly jail bait, and/or farm boy, and/or air-of-innocence, and/or any number of those thoroughly sexy images you project. So, we're not really competitors, you and I, although we're in the same business; although you're a mere dabbler, while I, by necessity, am the more serious businessman. So, while I'm no longer new meat, like you are; while I'm no longer young, like you are; while I'm no longer stupid enough to think that I'll hold to my regulars forever, accepting that someone younger, better-hung, and more tall-dark-and-handsome will someday soon supplant me, my customers will always be Jaguar buyers, while you're a well-tuned Porsche, or vice versa, if you know what I mean."

I feel foolish.

"That said," he continues, "I've, also, got the brains to know, now that you've had a bit more variety in your life, you probably don't find me nearly as good a catch as you might once have."

Is this handsome stud kidding, or what?

"I brought at least as much cash as you're asking these days. Even enough for if you charge me extra for having gotten to your ass, freebie, the first time."

"You're saying you'll pay to fuck me?"

"Wouldn't I be presumptuous to expect special treatment, just because of our first time?"

"You may think you chose me, but it was actually the other way around," I admit to him.

"You're certainly learning the subtle art of flattery, as well as ..."

"Flattery, my ass!" How can I like, so much, someone who comes off such a perfect jerk? "Out of a whole park of big cocks, and handsome faces, and studly bodies, I picked your cock, your face, and your body. I'm as eager for seconds, as you now pretend to be. I don't need the additional incentive of fifty-dollar bills waved in my face."

"Okay, okay," he concedes. "And a little story to prove I don't have to be knocked over the head twice. About this guy, actually me, back in the days when I first put a price tag on my dick. This one really nice trick, having paid in full for my services, decides he wants to give me an expensive watch. He doesn't want anything additional, he says. He just wants me to have it, because he likes me, he likes the watch, and he'd like me and the watch be together. I tell him no. I tell him no again. I'm suspicious of alternative motives, although don't ask me what those alternative motives were supposed to be. Finally, he says, 'Stud, you've got to learn just to accept what's offered, above and beyond the asking, and do so with a polite, sounds-sincere-even-if-it-isn't thank-you.' So, jail-bait, farm-boy, air-of-innocence Mr. Studly, accept my polite, sounds-sincere-because-it-is thank-you."

"Did you get the watch?"

"Naw, missed my chance. Which is why I don't want to miss my chance, this time around."

For me, there's often an awkward transition between finalizing dollars-to-be-paid-for-services dickering (even if that dollar-amount ends up zero), and the sex itself. The money-talk interrupts the as-I-see-it otherwise natural flow of meeting someone and, then, fucking, or getting fucked by him. For most of my paying customers, however, the bargaining with me, with anyone, is part of their fun, like buying a sombrero in Tijuana. One guy was so visibly disappointed when he couldn't get down my asking price, by even ten cents, he decided to pass on sex with me altogether. When he came around to try it again, he found I not only still wouldn't budge, but I'd raised my price, just for him. For some reason that got him hot as hell.

I don't know where Blue stands on liking, or not liking, his necessary bargainings over his own price as asked on Boyland Park's meat rack. Maybe every hustler, even me, eventually overcomes our childish notions of what should and shouldn't constitute perfect sex, because being asked, "How much?", and coming up with the answer, are part of the game being played.

If it bothers me all that much, I'd head to the other side of the park and enjoy sex without any monetary value attached to it.

Whether Blue is excited by his having offered cash, or by my having refused it, or both, or whether it was just a required chore gotten out of the way, he proceeds smoothly to the next step.

"Why don't you turn around again and give me another look-see of your fine young ass?" he says.

I oblige.

"Your cock looks good enough to eat, but your butt is something else again."

I've figured him so hung up on my ass being cherry the first time he'd fucked it that he'd never come around for seconds. The disappointment of wanting him again, when he likely wouldn't want me ever again, was one of the reasons I'd seen less of him since. Of course, my sudden shedding of inhibitions, in the aftermath of his cock exploded up my butt, saw me too busy experimenting with other cocks and asses to accept, all that much, how much I really wanted a return of Blue's cock up my asshole.

"Wearing no shoes should make it easier for you to step out of your pants and undershorts, this time," he says. "Why not give it a try?"

I step out of them, hook them with one foot, and kick them out of the way.

"Now for your T-shirt."

I add it to the pile.

"Now, I just take a moment to enjoy this naked, jail-bait, farm-boy, air-of-innocence, hustler-in-the-park, sex-for-hire, Jesus-fuck beautiful butt."

He shifts position in the chair. His hands splay across the firm globes of my ass and catch hold, like a squirrel taking hold of the gnarls of some tree trunk. His thumbs pass each other as they slide, from opposite sides, into the crack of my ass. He gently pulls open the depths of my crack, like a peach, for better viewing."

"Lovely sweat-dampened valley," he says. "Delicious golden pucker, with just a hint of hair in halo as reassurance that, despite your young looks, you have, indeed, reached puberty. I'm not a chicken hawk, after all, and it's disconcerting how a few quick licks of a razor would have you so completely hairless as to convince just about everyone you aren't even old enough to get a boner."

He licks my asscrack, at its top where it opens onto the base of my spine. His next lick is lower and overlaps the first. I shudder as he continues, one small area at a time, all of the way to where my ass drops away to the hang of my already contracting scrotum with my cum-filled balls.

He rolls his moist tongue and funnels its slipperiness through my sphincter, and I actually yelp like a goddamned bitch in heat and raise up on my toes.

"Delicious," he says after his tongue pulls out, and I'm left with an emptiness in my behind, as if his tongue had been hard and fucking cock that had prematurely pulled from its natural sheathe.

My dick, what with all its clear leakage, resembles one of those fountains in the park. It's so inviting, I decide to take a drink. Not so impossible, considering the size of my erect cock, and my dexterity from constant training in my high-school varsity gymnastics.

I lean forward and grab my legs just above the back of my knees.

"Yes, yes!" Blue is appreciative of the better view my positioning gives him of my asshole.

I suck in my stomach, hunch my shoulders, bow my head deeply, and zoom right in on my rock-solid dick. I suck in my bulbous cockhead.

"Jesus, kid, you sucking your own dick?" He's surprised. "Damn, you are, you lucky, lucky sonofabitch! Do you know how often I've tried to eat my own meat and failed by only a fraction of an inch?"

I could provide him with a few stretching exercises. I could oversee his training. I could be there the first time his mouth successfully closes over the tip of his erection and exerts the suction to dimple both his cheeks. Such are my fantasizes as I expertly suck ooze from my dick.

Even with as much workout as my cock sometimes gets in the park, I still, come home, on occasion, take a quick shower, and suck myself to climax. There's just something about getting sucked off, even by myself, that's totally different than when my cock wears a rubber. There's never been a time when I've sucked, or fucked, been sucked, or fucked, without the working cock being sheathed in latex. And, it's not because I haven't been asked. I had one guy down on his knees and begging for me to shoot my hot cum into his mouth. Crazy bastard! to risk it. Granted, he was safe enough with my cum, considering my precautions, but what if I hadn't been so careful? In the end, I jacked off and let him do his best to catch whatever my spraying cum he could, without his lips ever touching down. If he ended up with more of my cum splattered on his chest, neck and face, than he ever managed to swallow, he seemed perfectly content with the compromise. He even tipped me an additional ten.

"You're making me really hot and horny, kid," Blue says. "As if I didn't arrive here hot and horny."

Cort Forbes

His finger is at the opening of my ass. I know it's his finger, not his cock, because I've had the latter there before, and there's a world of difference. Which doesn't mean that, when he begins to screw his obviously spit-soaked finger up my behind, it doesn't bring with it it's own unique surge of pleasure. When Blue has my butt skewered to where his finger pokes my prostate, I drink the resulting gush that spills from the still-sucked head of my penis.

He cups my balls with his free hand and gives them a squeeze.

"Mmmmm," I hum appreciation.

I'm so hyped I'm going to have to be damned careful to avoid the kind of premature ejaculation that happened my first time with Blue. Not that that premature ejaculation prevented me from proceeding directly to an even more intensive orgasm, as provided by the skillful expertise of Blue's fucking dick. Not that a premature ejaculation, now, would likely mean I wouldn't proceed, non-stop, to orgasm, once I had his cock working its magic inside me. I just like to think I have a bit more control these days, and that ...

The climax hits me like a ton of bricks. Obviously, it has something to do with who I am, with who Blue is, with Blue looking as studly as he does, and with my finding him so much a sexual turn-on. All of that, plus how the sucking of my cock coincided with a violent twisting of Blue's finger against my prostate.

During my climax, my asshole opens wider around his finger, then collapses with the force of a vise around a steel rod. My hearty, heavy blasts of cum feed my face a five-course meal (I count each gooey serving), and follows up with a slow drool of exquisitely tasty dessert.

"All your fun and games in the park," Blue says, "and you still have the knack, don't you, to make it seem as if I'm getting to your ass for its very first time?"

I cease sucking my cock and look between my legs to see him on the other side.

"You've been a virile young stud from the get-go, haven't you?" he says. At the same time, he scoots out of his pants, even as he stays pretty much seated in the chair.

His impressive erection is suddenly in full-view.

"Look how stiff you make me, kid," he says, as if I haven't already noticed and been flattered. Carefully, he unrolls a condom over the tip of his uplifted length of meat.

"You have enough room to stand up?" I ask. It'll take a good foot of space, after he's standing to lower his cock, like castle drawbridge, to any convenient positioning at my pucker.

"If you can manage me just a bit more room." His hands, on my hips, provide additional balance as I, still bent over, give him what he needs to stand and get his cock properly aligned.

"Sorry if you were expecting more foreplay," he apologizes and puts his rubberized cockhead through my asscrack to my pucker. "You've just got me way too hot and bothered for any more of a lengthy lead-in."

I've had all the foreplay I need. I want his cock bored up my butt as much as he wants it there. Possibly I want it even more.

One thing we both correctly suspect: no need to be as careful, this time around, for fear his cock will split a cherry asshole. If my rectum is no less tight than it was when virgin (I've made comparisons by pushing my finger up there, both before and after the fact), I've learned a bit about muscle control, and ...

"Aggghrrr!" I grunt as he gives me everything he's got, which is one helluva lot, in one forceful and seemingly non-ending slide.

Cort Forbes

"Goddamn!" he says as his lower belly collides with my ass in an audible slap. Beneath the pressure of his muscled stomach, my asscheeks flatten. "I don't fucking believe ... This can't be happening! Jesus ... not to ... goddamn ... fucking ... me!"

He blasts off. No doubt about it. Rubberized or not, his cock, so firmly wedged inside me, pulses, pulses, pulses. If the wetness of his cum isn't physically spraying the bare interior of my asshole, there's no mistaking the additional space required by the ballooning tip of his rubber as it suddenly fills with each and every powerful gushings of hot and pearly cum he has to offer.

"Unbelievable!" he manages finally, his cock no longer pulsing, as if my asshole were a python whose swallowed-whole victim has finally stopped all struggle. "Believe me when I tell you I'm not usually so quick on the trigger. It's just that getting to your butt this second time has me riled like sex with no one else ever has."

"I'm flattered."

"Maybe, but if you were a paying customer, you'd likely ask for a refund of your money about now."

"Why? You aren't good for seconds?"

"Probably with you, where I wouldn't likely be with a regular john."

I doubt that, because I've seen his cock stay perfectly hard after having just blasted off up more than one guy's hot and spasming butt.

"I haven't lost control, like that, in years." He still can't quite forgive himself, although he'd been generous enough when I'd creamed, our first time, with his cock barely up my ass.

"I'll bet the farm you won't even lose your hard," I say. It's what, or very similar to what he'd said to me, that first time.

"You're probably right," he agrees, and I'm damned happy to hear it. "Except, I have to pull this excitable dick of mine out for re-vulcanization."

He isn't fishing for me to say, "Oh, for God's sake, take a chance and screw me just as you and your dick are. I'm willing to risk the danger of your cum-slimed rubber slipping off during phase two." He's always been careful about safeguards, and he's not about to make an exception for me.

He squeezes the base of his cock between an index and fuck finger. If his cock were a cigarette, the next step would be to lift its base to his mouth for a puff. It isn't a cigarette, though. It's a still-stiff prick, just having blasted its load, and it has a heavy bag of slippery jism attached, by latex, to its tip. His fingers vise the base of his cock, anchoring the lower extremely of the rubber and making sure the condom stays put as his dick slips out. There's an audible "plop" as the last of his cock exits my asshole.

He sits down to peel the used rubber off his erection.

I sit at his feet for a better look. I've never seen his cock up close and personal in such good lighting.

"Damn!" he complains, and I see he's caught a couple of his pubic hairs in rolled-up rubber, in his anxiousness to free his dick of the jism-sloshed container still balanced precariously atop his prick. "They should make these things a little less fond of plucking a guy's pubic hair."

"Want me to get soap and a razor before you don the next condom?" I ask. I imagine him without his curly bush of black crotch hair. Except for it, and the hair on his head, and possibly hair in the crack of his ass (where I've never peeked, but now have a rabid desire to do so), his body is hairless.

"You might enjoy shaving my scrotum and around the base

of my dick," he says. "I may well enjoy you shaving there. But, my paying customers would certainly bitch that if they wanted fucked by someone without pubic hair they would be out picking up chicken, fresh off some school yard."

"I'm way too fond of it to shave it anyway."

"Don't lay it on too thick, kid," he says, smiles, and looks at me as he does so. He's untangled his pubic hair from the rubber and has rolled the latex to where there's no farther chance of it snagging.

I watch the additional unveiling of his cock like a virgin straight guy probably watches, enraptured, a stripper. Nor am I any less excited by what I see than the straight guy would be when given a mouth-watering glimpse of some showgirl's pussy. I'm probably more excited, because Blue's cock is more of an eyeful than any mere slice of vacuous female cunt .

Like the rest of Blue, his cock is just about perfection. From top to bottom, it's an impressive missile, fattest at its base, with a gradual taper to a head that doesn't so much flare impressively, like mushroom cap from thick stem, but, rather, like gradual merging of finger (albeit a very thick, very large, very impressive finger), into fingertip. Whatever doctor performed the circumcision of Blue's cock, he'd done a flawless job that's left not a trace of webbing between cockhead and cockshaft. The resulting encirclement of scar tissue has, over the years, achieved the same mellow shade of gold as the uncut regions of his erection.

A few veins meander his cockshaft, close enough to the surface to provide a sexy filigree, but not so close as to show blue through the golden skin.

The used condom has come completely free, and Blue ties off its loose end and balances it on the arm of the chair. He bends for his pants presently pooled around his feet. I shift back slightly but not so far that I can't enjoy the brush of his cheek against mine, as he's on his way down.

While down, he removes both of his boots, so his return to a sitting position allows him his pants in his lap without their encasing his muscled legs in the process. From a front pocket of his jeans, he gets a handkerchief and another rubber. He puts the spent, cum-juiced condom into the pocket, like a good camper sure not to leave litter.

His hanky wipes his dick clean of whatever sticky residue might make the next rubber fit less securely than intended. Three times, he puts a fuck finger down beneath his balls, all of the way to where his fingertip is actually in his asshole, and presses as he drags that finger back up the corridor that is the roadway for cum from his impressive balls. His thumb, hooked around the base of his cock, joins with the pressing finger in milking an ooze of stale cum to be sopped up by his hanky.

When he's finished, to his approval, I say, "Let me put on the new rubber."

"Why not?" he agrees over the top of his cock. His prick suddenly slaps back against his stomach with the sound of a bat hitting a hardball.

I tear open the condom packet with my teeth, like I've seen him do. The latex is lubricated, and I taste its not-totally-unpleasant oil slick as I pinch the condom's nippled center into a more definable tent and cap the top of Blue's erection with it.

"Don't spend too much time," Blue says. "Not unless you want to take time for me to don rubber number three before I get my cock back up your sexy ass."

"You bring rubber number three, just in case?" I begin a slow unroll of the latex toward the thickest part of his erection.

"And a rubber number four and a rubber number five," he

says. "After which, we'll have to raid your supply."

"Happy to oblige," I say, and get even more turned on the longer I feel even a bit of his naked cock against my fingers. Oh, for those days, when people, not just gays, fucked and sucked, were fucked and sucked, without cloaking cock in rubber! Then again, how can I miss something I've never known? The fear of AIDS has made my whole sex life a rubberized affair, except for when my own mouth wraps my dick, or my own hand wraps my dick, or when I oblige the occasional willing hand of someone else wrapping my dick. Warm, bare asshole hugging hot, naked cock, I can only imagine as something else again. "There," I say, mission completed.

I'm not insulted that he gives my workmanship a quick once-over. After all, it's my asshole about to get fucked. Any accidents, and it's my butt flooded with potentially contaminated cum.

"So," he says, "do we give this one more try, or what?"

"Would you like me positioned as before?" I stand up, turn my butt toward him and bend over. I grab my asscheeks and tug them open, along their mutually shared crack. "What do you think?"

"I think: far too sexy for either of our own goods," he says and stands.

His feet, completely unfettered of his trousers, assume a wider stance than before as he advantages my pucker so readily put at his disposal.

"This going to be hard and fast, again, is it?" I ask.

"Keep you guessing," he says, his hands on my hips. "You, or anyone else, knowing what's about to happen next can be downright boring, don't you ..." He pushes half of his dick up my butt, hears my grunt, then completes with "... think?"

"Right!" My voice is downright breathless.

He pulls out half of the half of his cock he's placed inside me, then reinstates all of what he's freed plus half of what remains suspended between his crotch and my asshole.

"You just stuck your dick all of the way up into the base of my throat, from the inside, or am I imagining it?" Between my legs, against the pendulum swing of my balls-contracting scrotum, his hairy-bagged testicles brushes mine in a similar swing.

He doesn't answer but feeds me the rest of his erection with a buck of his hips that would topple me except for his hands at my hips for needed support and balance.

"How's it feel now?" he asks.

"Can't you tell your cockhead is laid out against the base of my tongue?"

We stay locked that way for a good minute. Maybe he knows I need the minute to pull myself together and reassure myself, once again, that my asshole hasn't undergone permanent damage under the assault of a cock as big as his. Then again, maybe ...

"What is there about this asshole of yours that puts me so close to blast-off by just poking full-length inside it?" he complains but doesn't really complain. "You a witch?"

"Maybe a warlock." I give my butt a little swivel to turn his cock inside me.

"Whatever, take the secret and patent it, kid. I'm a pro, and if you make such magic for me, you've got a fortune up your asshole."

"Funny, but it feels more like a genuinely gigantic cock up there," I beg to differ.

"That, too," he admits.

His hands slide forward and down the front of me. One continues between my legs and finds not only my nuts but his. Our four testicles get rolled sensuously against one another before our simultaneously contracting scrotums can hoist them out of reach. His other hand fists my dick.

"Holding tight to your prick gives me the illusion of my cock thrust all the way through you and out your other side," he says.

"You want to pretend my cock is your cock, as you whack mine off and fuck my ass, be my guest." It may seem like his dick to him, but I enjoy all the benefits from every stroke of his fingers.

His cock pulls outward. At the same time, his hand slides up my dick. He feeds his cock inward. At the same time, his hand slides down my dick.

Suddenly, he stops. His lap fully cups my behind. His cock is buried its full length inside me, so far in that my butt flattens against the pressure of his muscled lower belly.

"Let's see if I can surprise us and make this last," he says. He commences a slower fucking cadence: a long and easy withdrawal of his cock to its tip, a long and easy replacement of his total inches up my ass.

"I like it, I like it," I compliment not only his less frantic fucking but his slower, coordinated, pump of my hard cock.

Bent as I am, I see beneath my balls, my scrotum already a curtain halfway risen for Act I. His scrotum still swings slightly, forward-back, back-forward, but is in the process of compaction, too. Inside our hairy sacs, our nuts move with lives all their own, manoeuvring for new positions within fleshy walls that are collapsing in upon them.

If I make the attempt, I can possibly exaggerate my bend to put my head all of the way through the opening between my knees. Doing so will allow me to see the progression of Blue's cock in and out of my butt. I don't, though, because I'm merely flexible, not double-jointed, and that stretch isn't easily achieved. My effort might result in our being put off balance. And I like where we are, thank-you very much.

The curve of his torso melds to mine, like a setting molds to a gemstone. The smoothness of his cheek, as it presses my back, tells me he's recently shaved.

"Jesus, this is pure heaven." His lips are butterfly wings against my skin.

We've achieved a workable, sensuous rhythm. It slowly builds our passions while allowing us our equilibrium. I've a good view of my cock, slow-and-easy, easy-and-slow, fucking his hand. Each ride of my cock through his fist is all the way. The heel of his gripping hand grinds my pubic hair on each completed push of my prick through his fingers.

"However, I'm not going to make this last forever, am I?" he warns. His hand, not occupied with my cock, hooks one of my hipbones and takes a firm hold.

I'm torn between wanting it to last forever and wanting it to end immediately in a firestorm of pleasurable eruption. As ecstasy builds, the fuck gets better and better. Except, there's such a thing as too much of a good thing. There's a point, although this is one of the few times I've actually reached it, when pre-orgasmic ecstasy reaches such a high pitch that I wonder if it isn't actually more pain than pleasure.

"Good ... good ... good!" I want to convince myself that what I enjoy is genuine enjoyment.

"How close are you, kid?" His question is accompanied by his grunting against my back.

"Close," I admit. I've held off by the distraction of mentally doing the multiplication tables. Has he held off just because he's

Cort Forbes

waited for me to cum with him?

"You want control of your dick so we can coordinate our ... Jesus, I'm close!"

I don't want to take over flogging of my dick. He's doing just fine. If he's as close to blast-off as he says, I'll be right there with him when the time comes.

"I'm going to cream, kid," he confirms and sounds apologetic. "Soon. Too soon?"

"Not ... too ... soon," I assure him. I don't say more, because I, once again, suck my face to my dick. There's no way he sees me returned to eating my cock, but he knows.

"Yeah, eat your whenever-it-comes gooey spunk, kid," he says, his voice sexily raspy. "Suck your dick dry while I fill your asshole with gallons of ... sweet, sweet .... Jesus, sweet ... heavy ... heavy ... man-cream!"

He explodes up my butt at the same time the first of my jism empties into my mouth. I've suddenly so much cream ballooning my cheeks, the first of it is barely swallowed without spilling. There so much, in follow-up, I wonder if I'm not, somehow, miraculously, eating Blue's emptying load, as well as my own. Again, I swallow a mouthful.

The final, loud, slap of Blue's hard belly against my hard ass locks us in place, then keeps us locked. Blue grinds against my rear. The original tenting of rubber at the tip of his cock swells so much that it becomes an extension of his cock and makes me feel as if he's grown an additional inch of meat inside me.

What happens next takes merely seconds, but time obliges by slowing down. There's a slow-motion quality to our orgasms that I've never experienced before, and I doubt I'll ever have the pleasure of frequently experiencing again. The waves of pleasure don't miss even one part of my body.

It's disconcerting how one stud, Blue, is the source of so much exquisite pleasure. If our first time together was good, and it was ... If this time is even better, and it is ... Dare either of us risk any further repeats for fear of expecting too much from a spiralling of available sensations that may have already reached its zenith and topped out there?

He moans his appreciation, then says: "Goddamn."

I want him to leave his now fully exploded cock inside me, in that it seems an integral part of my guts. To pull it free will be to remove something from me that's vital for my very existence.

I'm glad, though, Blue has sense enough to recognize the possible danger of his cum-filled rubber left inside me, as his cock finally begins softening for a more easy shedding of its rubberized packaging.

Blue anchors the latex firmly to the base of his cock, to prevent any spillage, and he pulls his dick and its cum-sopped container free of my butt. The tip of his condom is so ballooned, with his exploded goo, my asshole, shutting tightly behind his exiting dick, threatens a vising that'll pop that balloon.

Luckily, his cock and its full condom pull out all the way without mishap. Nothing is left in my asshole but the veneer of lubricant my anal lining has scraped from the rubber, and the residual ecstasy of my having spasmed so violently when skewered on Blue's cum-spewing cock.

He ties off the rubber and gives it a toss. It makes a sloshy sound as gravity converts it to an opaque pool on the chair seat. Blue's hands slide around me, up my belly, and finally cup my pecs. He leans in close to my ear, his head bowed over one of my sweaty shoulders.

"So fine!" He tells me nothing I don't already know. "Makes me wonder ..."

I have to probe for the rest of his interrupted thought. "Makes you wonder what?"

After a pregnant pause: "Wonder how it would be with your stiff cock fucked up my butt."

Does he know my cock has already been there, if only in my wildest, wettest dreams?

"Think you'd like to fuck my ass?" He has to ask? "I might like it," he continues. "Really like it. Not here, and not now, because I want time to savor the memory and aftermath of this fuck. Maybe tomorrow? In Boyland Park, for old-time's sake? Me handcuffed to a tree stump, and you beating my ass with a paddle before sticking your hard dick, slow and deep up my asshole?"

I don't turn to face him. "You're kidding, right?" Hopefully, not about my cock up his butt, because I can't think of anything I want more. But him bent over a tree stump? My paddling his ass?

"You could do that for me, couldn't you, kid?"

"I know a black man who can do it for you a helluva lot better and pay you for the privilege." I want to fuck Blue. Jesus, I want to fuck him! But, why does he need the kinkiness of handcuffs and paddle when we both get such a high without them? "You need someone who knows what he's doing when you get involved in that B&D bullshit."

"You've been under the paddle." His mouth is closer to my ear and tickles. "Who better for me to have on the delivery end of paddle and hard cock?"

"Jesus, Blue!" I sound as disappointed by the complications as I am.

"I don't want the black man my first time, kid," Blue says. "Maybe later, sure, but not my first. My first should be with someone special, like I was special for you, your first time. Yes?"

Is he talking first time handcuffed and paddled, or is he talking something else? It seems too impossible that ...

"Surprised my ass is still cherry?" he makes valid my wildest flight of fancy.

Of course I'm surprised!

"You hustlers, nowadays, are a more enlightened breed. Hustlers from my generation, more often than not, can get our cocks sucked, and our cocks fucked into any number of asshole, from here to China, but its an unwritten rule that we don't get fucked, and we don't kiss. You ever let one of your johns kiss you, kid?"

"Once." He'd been cute. So cute, I'd almost fucked him for free. I'd recognized him from a rival high school. He said his name was John: john John , which I, somehow, found extremely amusing at the time.

"I've never kissed a man, kid. Hell, your butt is the first butt I've ever kissed. Oh, I've had countless mouths and asses swinging on my dick, but that's it. You want my first homo kiss on the mouth, too?"

I turn in his arms. I want to see his face. I want to see for myself, read in his eyes and expression, that he's not feeding me a load of bullshit to rival the load of cum his rubberized cock has so recently pumped up my ass.

"I'm prepared to lose old inhibitions," he says. "With you, anything is possible."

He's so close, so sexy. His lips are full, desirable, inviting. He licks them, and his mouth is all the more sensuous when wet.

My fingers run into the black hair on either side of his head. I step closer and expect him to back away, but he stays firm, right where he is. Our chests and bellies touch, his nipples hard against my chest, my nipples hard against his. Our cocks jockey for position, one banging sexily against the other, within the small space left between us.

I want to kiss him. I want to be kissed by him. I want to fuck him. Fucking him now would be perfect, but I'm prepared to wait until tomorrow if that's what he wants. I'll fuck him in the park, on a busy street, hanging upside-down from a lamp post, if that's how he wants it . However, there remains something about his additional request for handcuffs and paddle that continues to leave me uneasy. Maybe because my experience with the black man left me promising myself I would never do it again. Would putting myself on the other end of the paddle, on the other end of the cock, really be breaking my promise?

Blue's hands parenthesize my face. His wet lips open slightly. Can virgin lips look so inviting?

Our mouths touch and send a thrill that electrifies all of the way to my toes. My lips open slightly against his. Do virgin lips know how to kiss, as Blue's lips so obviously know how to kiss? Then again, he's emphasized mine is the first kiss he's had from a man. Have there been kisses of women, then? Lots of them? I know so bloody little about Blue's past, or about what he does when he's not at the park.

Ours is a nice, sexy, first kiss. Neither of us make any move to swallow each other's tongue or whole face. It's the kind of kiss I actually prefer, instead of being threatened with drowning in a sudden exchange of saliva.

"About your virgin ass," I say when the kiss, to my regret, is finally over and done. "Wouldn't you prefer to break it in slowly, maybe move on to handcuffs and paddle later?"

"Not really."

"Then, it's handcuffs, paddle, virgin ass, or nothing at all?"

"You're that set against whacking my cherry ass with a plank?"

Am I? After all, it's not me who'll end up with the bruises this time.

"I'll even supply the handcuffs and paddle," he entices.

"Did I miss you confirm this as an all or nothing proposition?"

"It's probably not, but ..."

"But?"

"I've kind of been working on this major fantasy: you, your cock, handcuffs, a paddle, my cherry ass. I'll have to revise that fantasy, but I suppose it's possible. If I really have to."

"Oh, hell!" So, what if I am a pushover? He and his fantasy are simply too much for a poor, horny boy like me to resist.

His cock and mine go soft in the aftermath of our fuck. While we dress, though, they return to rock-hardness. Neither of us suggests we try for an immediate additional fuck. I would love a crack at Blue's studly ass, right then and there, whether it's cherry or not, but he's so determined for B&D in the park, the next evening, I don't risk a move for fear of a rebuff.

I keep my woody until three o'clock in the morning, when I finally beat off or risk a bad case of blue balls (a condition surprisingly well-named, considering the circumstances).

I have another raging boner when I wake up later the same morning. It's so visible in my pants, after I dress, I expect my mother to make some uncharacteristic comment about it. Luckily, she's running late for a hair appointment. Sex isn't a subject in which mom ever seems particularly interested. If pressed, she'll blame dad for having screwed her so badly, literally and figuratively, before leaving her with me as a one-year-old baby.

Cort Forbes

When I meet Blue at the east entrance to the park, his cock is no less impressively displayed than mine. We recognize our shared stiff-cock condition, at one and the same time, and exchange would-you-believe-this-? smiles.

"Having to lug around this boner all day makes me more sympathetic to women nine-month's pregnant," he says.

If I think my dick will soften, the closer we get to what we're about that evening, I'm dead wrong. As we take the shortest route to where we're headed, my cock actually gets stiffer.

We're en route to the same spot where the black man bent me over a tree stump, handcuffed my wrists to a convenient upthrust of tree root, whacked my ass with a paddle, then fucked me. There's no better locale I can think of that's more suitable for our purpose. I wonder how long it took the black man to locate the spot, or if he, first, found the spot and, then, figured out how best to use it.

"So, here we are," Blue says.

We're in a natural depression, surrounded by a dense growth of trees. The stump, cut to about my mid-thigh, has center stage. I've no idea why this one tree is cut down, the bulk of its trunk hauled away. I doubt the black man did the deed, just to fit his particular needs. The cutting looks old. A thick growth of moss covers the rotten bark.

"Handcuffs," Blue says and produces them from the gym bag he carries.

I know the locks are broken, because they're broken on the Black man's pair.

I'm not concerned the black man may show and be ticked with us for usurping his favorite spot. The black man keeps a rigid schedule. He shows on the first and third Wednesdays of every month. Never on a Monday, never on a Tuesday...

Always Wednesday. Never two Wednesdays in a row, either. He's not due for another week.

"Paddle," Blue needlessly identifies his latest rabbit-from-the-bag trick.

It's one of those fraternity paddles used for paddling freshmen ass. Meandering around its holes there's the Greek name of a frat at a local college.

I remain uneasy about what we're up to, but Blue seems perfectly at ease. Our playthings unbagged, Blue begins to strip.

I was less nervous when I agreed to the session with the black man. This should be easier, but I can't help wonder if Blue knows what he's letting himself in for. Does he expect me to go easy on him, or does he really expect me to put the same force behind the paddle that the black man does?

Blue doesn't comment on the slowness of my striptease. When he's buck naked, his hard dick upthrust like some Priapic shrine, he sits on the tree stump and waits patiently for me to catch up.

Eventually, I'm naked, handcuffs in-hand. Without hesitation, Blue rolls to his belly on the stump. His legs hang over one end, his head and arms hang over the other. He puts his wrists exactly where the handcuffs, one bracelet to one wrist, can be successfully threaded through a upbowed bit of root before attachment of the other bracelet to Blue's other wrist.

Suddenly, I'm excited as hell by him, cuffed, naked, and seemingly vulnerable. I see where the black man gets his jollies on the delivering end of paddle and cock. There's something deliciously inviting about Blue's virgin butt so willing to be paddled, then fucked.

The paddle is heavy but well-balanced. Dark stains on its wood give evidence of asses hit hard enough to bleed.

Cort Forbes

I stand behind and slightly to one side of Blue's butt. How does his hard cock fare between the press of his hard belly and the unyielding support of the tree-stump? I can't remember if my boner, so positioned during my ass being beaten and fucked by the black man, caused me discomfort.

I connect paddle to ass, the wood to naked buttocks sending a shock wave the my entire length of arm. There's a lingering vibration of the wood against butt before the paddle drops away. Blue's asscheeks are immediately polka-dotted with dark circles that match the pattern of holes in the paddle.

"You've been a naughty cocksucker, haven't you?" I say to Blue, because that's what the black man said, after the first paddle blow. "You make me beat your ass, even though I don't want to."

My second placement of wood to ass is harder, because I'm suddenly resentful Blue puts me in this position of not only doing something I thought I'd never do but makes me realize I enjoy it.

The two dull thuds of paddle to Blue's butt remind me of another reason the spot is so perfect. Its acoustics muffle sounds. There's virtually no echo.

"You want punished for being such a shit, don't you." I don't make it a question, just like in the black man's original script. "Tell me you want it, need it, in order to feel adequately chastised."

"Yes," says Blue.

His butt has to be hurting. Polka-dots of the second whack has overlapped polka-dots of the first. The taut flesh between all the polka-dots is shaded differently than when the spanking began.

"Tell me how much you want and need another whack to make you all the more a better boy."

"Yes, please."

He gets his wish. I can't see the expressions on his face, because his face is turned away. I don't like hurting him. I don't like enjoying hurting him. I thought my guilty conscious would make my dick shrink so far I'd have trouble finding it. But, here I am, on the verge of whack three, and my cock is so stiff it would probably shatter if hit by a silver spoon.

"Let me hear you say please, again, you naughty, naughty bastard. Let me know you're mending your disgusting ways."

"Please, spank me," Blue says and even sounds sincere. Had my performance, with the black man, been anywhere as good?

"Good boy," I say and deliver paddle to ass for a third and final time

The black man never slaps ass more nor less than three times. Will a fourth draw blood and threaten permanent damage?

"One more time, please," Blue says. It's not part of the script.

"What do you mean, one more time?" I ask, angry. Why am I so fucking angry?

He turns his face so I see it, and I shift for an even better look.

"I want to make sure you haven't gone easy on me," he says, "because I've been a very naughty boy and deserve full punishment."

"What bullshit!" I accuse. Have I gone easy on him, afraid I'll hurt him? Unsure of myself, unlike the black man who's learned from trial and error, have I whipped Blue's ass and erred on the side of caution? Does Blue knowing I've done so make me as angry as I suddenly am?

"I want it, please, sir," he says. His eyes squint, but he looks right at me. "Please," he repeats. "I want to be better, and I need to know the consequences of being so naughty."

"You fucking, masochistic shit!"

"Spare the rod, spoil the child," he says. He's actually smiling.

"Spare the rod?" For not the first time, I'm Polly-want-a-cracker parrot. "Spoil the child? You want that studly ass of yours spoiled for good? Want it to bleed? Want nasty scars instead of just black and blue marks?"

"Just one more time," he says. "You wouldn't want it said that you played favorites. You wouldn't want some naughty little shit, come after me, to complain how I was let off easy."

I grip the handle of the paddle so hard it hurts.

"The others will say you've gone soft," he continues. "Lost the touch. No longer have the knack, the will to be a good disciplinarian. Couldn't adequately paddle ass if you had to."

I tell myself to drop the paddle and walk away. Leave Blue to whatever his sick fantasies. Tell him to wait for the black man who knows a helluva lot more about ass beating than I ever will.

Instead, I move determinedly back into convenient striking distance and deliver a fourth whack that convinces Blue and me that I'm not holding back anything — this time. The blow is so hard it gets a rare echo. My whole arm, from fingertips to shoulder, goes numb.

When the paddle falls away ...

"Jesus, blood!" I drop the paddle. I drop to my knees. His paddle-damaged ass a pagan altar at which I kneel to beg forgiveness. "You've made me hurt you, you bastard!"

Where several polka-dots have overlapped, the shared skin has broken. On closer look, it's not serious, but that doesn't make me any less a shit.

In safer, pre-AIDS days, I would kiss the spot, to make it better. Might even lap up the spilled blood and enjoy its salty, slightly metallic taste. Now, all I do is wipe the blood away with the flat of my hand, glad coagulation already stops the flow.

"Damn it!" I say and put my cheek to a section of his ass that doesn't bleed. His buttocks is hot as hell.

"You haven't killed me, kid" Blue reminds. "My ass no less cherry for a beating your black man would be hard-pressed to match."

"He's not my black man," I emphasize the possessive.

"Of more importance, to us, my ass is still cherry and ripe for fucking."

"Jesus, Blue ... " I protest.

"Your cock suddenly limp?" He answers his own question. "Naw. Nor is mine. So, we should move right along to the really good part."

As much as my concern remains, as to the possible damage I've done his ass, I still want to fuck him, here and now, more than I've ever wanted anything. My desire all the greater in his having chosen me.

"You going to fuck me, or what?"

"I'm going to fuck you," I say, but he's known it all along.

I'm still on my knees, face against his butt, but I pull back. I hook my thumbs into the cleft of his cherry buttocks, as if about to open a large, delicious peach along a convenient vertical slit. Within the crevice of his ass grows a line of dark hair, gone sweaty, punctuated by the surprisingly small hole to his rectum.

He doesn't remind me to go easy. Maybe he expects too much of me, because I wonder if I'm up to the task. What experience, after all, do I have in fucking cherry ass? All the assholes

Cort Forbes

I've screwed have been familiar with cock, long before mine took a peek. If I were a little quick on those insertions, a little rough during the course of those fucks, it didn't matter. But my only experience with virgin ass is Blue's fucking of mine. When he had, he'd come at it with years of experience in butt-fucking. Years that included, I'm sure, his plugging more than one virgin butt, lest how did he know he had such a fondness for it?

As flattered as I am, as excited as I am, to be the first to explore the tightness of Blue's ass, has Blue made a mistake in handing over his deflowering to a rank amateur? Without proper control, my cock, presently a raging boner, can do his cherry ass extensive damage, conceivably split it from the base of Blue's spine to the hang of Blue's hair-fuzzed balls.

My nose and face are at his asscrack, as if to don a gas mask when suddenly threatened by biological warfare. The tip of my nose prods his sphincter as my cock soon will. His asscheeks close in on my cheeks. I sniff his manly, musky smells, and my cock drools all the more. I'm so lost within the aphrodisiacal odors from his asshole, I'm amazed I remember a condom is needed before any fuck begins. It scares me that, for not the first time, I've almost forgotten the need for a protective layer of rubber between us, where Blue and I are concerned. Probably, he would remind me before letting my cock up his ass, but I'm supposedly the one in charge. Blue should be free to enjoy the ecstasy of my cock pushing slow and easy up his behind, not worry about whether or not I've got the brains to take the safety precautions necessary to protect the both of us.

I scramble for my pants. The black man was better prepared, having more conveniently placed his rubber beforehand.

I'm so nervous, I almost forget to wipe my cock clean of its present drool. Without the wipe-down, my cock will slip within any rubber, no matter how tightly the rubber might initially seem wrapped around it. A rubber so loosely anchored can slip off during any fuck.

The condom is so slippery with its own lubricant, it almost slips free of my fingers. Somehow, I tent it atop my prick and unfurl it to my balls.

All the while, Blue doesn't say a thing. Can he only endure the pain from his paddled butt, his asscheeks hot and discolored?

I stand and pry open his asshole once again to re-discover that fine line of black hair and the small rosebud hidden within them. When the time comes, all I'll have to do is walk up, my cock pulled down and take aim on his asshole. Then, just keep on walking until my belly flattens his buttocks, my cock long-gone up his ass. I'll have to make it a slow walk, of course. I'll have to pause, a few times, for his ass to adjust to my plugging of it. His asshole is only used to something as big as my cock when his asshole shits turds. Nothing so large and impressive has ever been offered the opportunity to journey in the opposite direction.

Blue says my name.

"I'm okay," I assure, whether he's asking or not.

My left hand is a wedge that enters his asscrack from the top and keeps the crack open and its pucker revealed. His sphincter is a bull's-eye, my stiff dick aimed right at it. My cock is pulled down from its upthrust before my belly, and its head pushes hard enough against his sphincter that, if pressed farther, will make his rectum roll-open for it.

"Cherry ass," I say and still can't believe it.

"Yours for the picking," Blue invites and rears so he, not I, feeds the first of my cock up his oh-so-tight behind.

Cort Forbes

"Christ, Blue!" I'm saying that I hope he's done the right thing, by him and by his asshole, to put my not-all-that-experienced cock in position for fucking his asshole.

"I want it, kid," he encourages. "I've wanted it from the start. Do you remember the first time you showed me your dick after watching me fuck in the park? I do. You waited until I was through, until you thought I was gone. Didn't know I circled around. Didn't know I jerked off, right along with you, only a few feet away, as you fed your hot and heavy load to the ferns."

His asshole is so tight around the head of my dick, it's as if I have a clothespin, or snapping turtle, clamped there. Sweet Jesus, how can either of us expect all of my cock to get inside him? Except, his cock is bigger than mine and entered my cherry ass-gone-cockless-before-it. Is Blue's asshole any the less adaptable?

He grunts softly as I ease another inch up his hot, clinging butt, then pause to let it rest there.

"More, kid," he invites. "I'll tell you if and when it gets to be too much ."

I'm reluctant, though, to move faster. Slip into higher gear, and I doubt I'll have the willpower to downshift if and when he should warn that his ass is about to split under the strain of my entering erection.

I decide it won't hurt to give him a little more, which is exactly what I do.

I would be more assured of painless success if we'd come at this like he and I fucked the first time: virgin asshole sitting down over hard cock at its own good speed. This way, I control the fuck, not Blue, not Blue's cherry ass. If I get carried away, no way will Blue get uncuffed, faulty lock or not, and get his ass unstuck before my fucking dick wreaks all kinds of damage to his

– 76 –

already paddle-damaged ass.

"I want all your cock inside of me," Blue says. Doesn't the handsome bastard know that the problem is just how much I, too, want my cock buried inside him? I really don't know if I've the willpower to pull this fuck off with the finesse it so definitely needs to be successful.

He does have the advantage of having fucked enough ass, virgin and otherwise, to know, at least from the delivering end, how asshole responds to penile penetration. Although such knowledge doesn't assure, one-hundred percent, his ability to make his own asshole open easily for any such penile penetration.

My dick is enough up his butt so that it no longer needs my supporting hand for guidance. Both my hands curve his hips for better support. Simultaneously, my cock eases even deeper inside him.

I worry that the night air evaporates the rubber's oily slick before it can do the job required in sliding my cock completely into place.

Another inch of my cock disappears up his ass before I know it. I pause, scared shitless by how quickly my dick proceeded inward without my really having had one iota of conscious say in the matter. It will be far safer for Blue, and for Blue's ass, if I pull out, here and now, and tell him to get his cherry ass broken in my someone who knows better how to go about it. Except, that isn't going to happen. Whatever cock I've fed him is too much for me to pull free before the deed is done. Whether I manage to do it right or not, whether Blue lives to regret my doing it or not, it's going to be my cock first fucked, tip to nuts, up his virgin rectum. To prove my point, I carefully feed more of my dick inside and pray to God I don't experience premature ejaculation, this time around, that will require me to pull out and re-sheathe, mid-fuck. Blue might have the control to pull his prematurely ejaculated cock out of my butt, in order to provide it with a fresh condom, but my managing such a feat is so far-fetched I can only concentrate on saving my climax for later.

Therefore, my pauses aren't so much my attempts to let Blue's virgin ass adjust to my sticking, although they certainly achieve that purpose, but are more my way of giving myself control over my building passion before I proceed to the placement of more cock up Blue's sexy behind.

I confess to some kind of self-hypnotic state, and I proceed, along my merry way, more and more of my cock up Blue's ass. Somehow, I manage, all the while, to keep my pleasure under control, and simultaneously keep his asshole in one piece. Actually, I'm surprised when I try to push more of my cock inside him, and realize I've no more cock to give him.

"Unbelievable!" I say, but the word is inadequate to express how much I marvel over the miracle.

I shake my head to clear it, afraid I've reached this magic moment by having ignored pleadings Blue may have made, gone unheard, in those final moments of my cock losing itself completely up his butt. I remember how even Blue, with all of his vast experience, all of his vast control, had been helpless to control his bucking of the last inch of his cock up my ass, when he'd taken my cherry.

"You okay?" I ask, but I don't want to hear if he's not okay. Split ass or not, I'm compelled to fuck it. I've neither the inner strength, nor the fortitude, to turn gentleman now, and say, "Sorry for whatever the inconvenience, buddy," and pull out and walk away.

He says, "I've never felt better, kid, except maybe when my

cock was buried to my balls up your cherry butt."

If he's okay now, I'm confident he'll be okay for however long the rest of my ride. From personal experience, I know a butt, once it knows a cock, is less shocked by its return. Whether that return comes another day, or whether it occurs after the mere withdrawal to cockhead, as I now do now before replacing all of my dick up his clutching butt.

"Yes," he says. In pleasure? In compliment?

How quickly we move, as one, into a sensuous fucking rhythm. His ass actually rises to meet each of my thrusts, then falls away to more quickly see my cock withdrawn to its head. Once, twice ... ten times ... twenty ... until I'm amazed how I somehow master the constant struggle to prevent my eruption into orgasm and, instead, achieve one more push up Blue's tight asshole.

"So good, so good, so good," he chants softly, sexily, each time my dick pokes his prostate and slides in to an even greater depth.

"Fuck you, fuck you, fuck you," I harmonize.

Our words become as intermingled as our bodies, as I come to know this fuck is just about over and done. I've expended all my capacity for making this fuck last as long as it can.

"Make me cum, kid!" Blue pleads, and if that's to be a reality, his orgasm has to be now. I'm at the top of the mountain with nowhere to go but ...

"Sorry," I apologize, because I so desperately want to keep fucking until I'm sure his balls are squirting in eruption. No matter what I want, though, or what Blue wants, my nuts demand immediate release of the hot and heavy cream contained within them, and they won't be denied. "Sorry!" I repeat and surrender to the exquisite, supreme pleasure. I surrender to some primitive control center somewhere inside of me that allows me no conscious say over what happens next.

I think my whole insides are liquid, siphoned downward into my already filled-to-capacity balls, to gush through my pulsing cock and fill the condom I've shoved so deeply up Blue's butt.

I grind my belly hard against the bruised surface of his twin-globed ass, and I shoot virtual gallons of creamy spunk.

Only later, when he's uncuffed, and unbends from his position over the stump, do I see proof he's not been short-changed in the matter. The stump is awash with his pearly slime. His pubic hair is sopped and tangled within a webbing of his exploded cream. His belly is slicked with his copious sexual discharge.

It's a couple of weeks before I'm back in the park and again seeking out Blue. I tell myself the interim is caused by how busy I've been getting re-acquainted with my father who's back in my life after seventeen years. I'm fooling myself, though. I've held back, because my first sex with Blue was so very good, my second sex with him was so very much better, and I fear any additional sex with him will be all downhill. Too many times, memories of a good time are spoiled by not-so-good repeats. Of course, I tell myself, if Blue had been all that anxious to see me, he knew where I lived, where I don't know squat about him, except he provides a good fuck, whether on the delivering or receiving end of hard cock.

I'm back in the park, headed for Blue, because I can't help myself. I want him, again, so badly that I'm willing to risk disappointment. I'm even willing to risk his, "Sorry, kid." I'm even prepared to pay him for sex with him, like everyone else.

He's there, thank-God alone, within the deeper shadows beneath his favorite tree.

"I thought you may have died and gone to heaven," I say and

know my definition of heaven includes his cock up my butt, or my cock up his rectum.

Except, it isn't Blue, after all. I see that now.

"Sorry! Thought you were someone else."

This stud's hair is dark, but not as blue-black as Blue's hair. This stud is handsome, but not nearly as handsome as Blue. This stud's bare torso is muscled, but not as exquisitely muscled as Blue's torso. The bulge this stud's cock makes in his jeans is impressive, but not nearly as impressive as the bulge Blue's cock makes in Blue's jeans.

"You thought I was Gregory," he says, and I can't decide if he's made it a question.

"Gregory?"

"The stud who usually hangs out here. Dark hair, like mine. Handsome as all hell. Big cock and all the skills to make getting fucked by it something you're not likely to forget."

"Yeah, Gregory."

His description of Blue is right on target. Obviously, Gregory is the name Blue uses with this stud.

"Gregory owes me a couple of bucks," I say. It's a lie, and don't ask me why, but I'm not ready to admit I'm here because of Blue's big cock and all the skills Blue uses to make my getting fucked (and my fucking him) something I can't forget.

"Well, I've some good news and some bad news," the guy at the tree says and rubs the ridge his dick makes in his pants. "The good news is that I figure Gregory is suddenly as well off, financially, as he's been in a very long time; so, he'll probably have whatever the cash he owes you. The bad news is that his sudden financial windfall is because he's run off with some black man who pays big time to whip and fuck Gregory's ass every other Wednesday."

"You're serious?"

"Yep!" He steps in closer. The heat of the day, lasted well into this evening, paints his tanned torso with an attractive gloss of sweat. "I guess the two really hit it off. Rumor is, the black man has been looking for a steady someone to play whipping post for quite sometime now, but no one ever quite fit the bill — until Gregory. The black man, I guess, has been after Gregory's ass for quite sometime now, and has put him up in some fancy pad uptown."

To say I'm surprised is the understatement of this year and next.

"No need for us not to capitalize on Gregory's good fortune, is there?" he asks.

I'm so involved with thoughts of Blue, or Gregory, or whomever the hell he is, suddenly gone from my life for good, I'm slow in picking up with where this stud is going.

"You and me," he's willing to spell it out for me. "Your obviously hard cock. My obviously willing asshole. Here and now. The right dollar amount in my trousers, I'd make bet." He quotes the dollar-amount he thinks I'd be asking, and he's not that far off. "I mean, if you aren't here to get fucked by Blue, but only to collect money from him, that tells me ..."

"Tells you what?" I want him to spell it out.

"That whatever the monster bulging your pants, it may be for sale."

"If it is?"

"I can think of nowhere I'd rather have it than fucked up my ass."

He deals dollars into the extended open palm of my hand, then he adds an extra large-denomination bill for good measure.

"Actually," he says, "I've seen you around and have been

tempted to give you a try for some time now. It's just that I knew what I got with Gregory, and it was always too damned good to resist, as long as it was available."

"Well, Gregory is off playing house with some black sadist," I say, "and I'm here to pick up the slack."

"What should I call you, kid?" he asks. "Anyone who gets as personal as putting his cock up my ass should have a name."

"Who would you like me to be for you, tonight, buddy?" I've heard Blue use that line plenty of times. It works for me.

The guy smiles. "You look like a Timmy," he says.

"So, Timmy it is," I comply.

"And I'm Garth. Like the rolly-polly cowboy singer, although there isn't anything even rolly-polly about me. I'm nothing but hard muscle, including my big cock and steely assbuns."

"Okay, Garth." I fold the money and slip it into my back pants pocket.

We both drop our pants, and I fuck the studly bastard until he squeals.

PERFORMING ARTS

Singleton Murray liked to watch attractive young men jack-off. More particularly, he liked to watch Art Monroe jack-off.

Art was strawberry blond and tanned: a lethal combination.

His hair was just long enough to feather the tops of both ears, and it banged his forehead in an attractive leftward sweep. His light green eyes didn't quite match the duller greens of his khaki T-shirt and tailored camouflage pants, but they were emphasized by them. Dog tags, with rubber silencers, hung from his neck, and his combat boots were spit-polished black, but Art's obvious youth made it doubtful he'd ever really served in the military.

His was a nice body. A trim body. The sleekness of a swimmer, as opposed to the skinniness of a runner, or the bulk of a gymnast.

A big cock.

"I'm going to come!" Art said and gave decided, breathless, little grunts: "Uggghh ... ughhh... ughhhhgh!"

Great gloppy gobs of Art's cum exited the wetly pouted mouth of Art's cockhead, then succumbed to gravity and crash-landed on the ground, on the moss along the ground, on the ferns grown from the ground.

"Excellent," Singleton said but, as far as he was concerned, the excellence was over and done, until he was alone in his room and could examine each and every aspect of Art's masturbatory performance in mental replay.

Singleton quickly made his exit, along one of the side paths that led to the parking spots along the periphery of Boyland Park.

Art stuffed his dick and balls back into his pants and noticed movement out of the corner of his eye.

"Shit!" he said. Which wasn't disappointed in seeing Gabriel Taylor. It was disappointment in not having spotted Gabriel before Art's cock had blasted for even the once that evening.

Brown-haired, blue-eyed Gabriel was bulky, like a body builder was bulky. He didn't look quite right in clothes, or out of them. Not that Art had ever seen Gabriel completely naked. Gabriel in a pair of crotch-bulged swimming trunks was just about as close as Art had ever come.

"Parker would like to see you," Gabriel said. "Since he's not wrapping the movie shoot until Tuesday, he hopes to see you, say Wednesday."

Art would be sure to have a full cock by Wednesday. "I'd like to see him, too."

On Wednesday, six sharp, the limo arrived outside Art's apartment, the money-bulged envelope right along with it.

Art got in, dressed cowboy, because Parker Crayne liked Art dressed cowboy.

Parker Crayne hadn't been Parker Crayne for the first eighteen years of his life but, rather, the butterball fat kid Greer Artman, or as he'd been called none too fondly by his classmates, who'd found his obesity gross, and his one helplessly loud fart, in the classroom, after an unfortunate breakfast of way too much bran, equally gross: Queer Greer Artman Fartman Fat Boy. Greer Artman had become a jettisoned name, along with all the fat, and most of the recalcitrant farting, when, at eighteen,

the adolescent kid had suddenly, quite miraculously, metamorphosed into a incredibly attractive young man. Suddenly, Parker
had cheekbones, hipbones, a jawline, a dimpled chin.
Suddenly, all the time and effort he'd put into trying to exercise
off his blubber did him proud by emerging, from beneath the
quickly dissolved body fat, as more than enough delineation to
provide the young man, augmented by his baby-blue eyes, tou-
sled black hair, and pouty pink lips, with a genuine air of raw sex-
uality.

So suddenly had this physical transformation occurred, so
quickly thereafter recognized by film producer Judd Clandy as
having the potential to come across eye-catchingly box-office on
the silver screen, Parker's mental transformation hadn't kept
pace. Any minute, he expected all the present wonder to disap-
pear, including his new name, his newly acquired fortune, and all
the adulation heaped upon him by his fawning movie-going pub-
lic.

When Parker personally opened the door of his penthouse
to admit Art Monroe, he greeted someone Parker thought
undoubtedly the most handsome stud Parker, bar none, had
ever seen, and that included all the movie stars with whom
Parker had had a chance to mingle since his debut in the block-
buster sci-fi western "Fort Danya-V". What's more, Parker suspected Art Monroe had never been unattractive, or fat, or fart-
prone, a whole day in Art's attractively thin and fartless life, let
alone suffered the cruel slings and arrows of vindictive school
kids whose tolerance for anyone even slightly different from
them was next to zero.

"Looking good!" Parker said and meant every word. If possible, Art looked better, each and every time Gabriel summoned
him to Parker's door. "Want something to drink?"

"Right now, all I want is your cock riding up my ass."

Where many a hustler guarded access to his asshole, like a miser guarded his cash, Art had never had any such hang-up.

"I'd like to fuck your ass," Parker said, no less amazed now than when he'd first been told by Gabriel that Art would actually let Parker fuck his butt. Just the thought of fucking Art's muscled rear end was all that had gotten Parker through the just-wrapped and exceptionally difficult movie shoot. Of all the butt Parker had fucked since he'd first fucked Art's asshole, and there had been more than a few, so many offered that it had been human-ly impossible for Parker to resist them all, the greatest pleasure that Parker had ever known was still what his cock had discov-ered within the asshole Art brought with him, every time, through Parker's penthouse door. "On the bed? On the floor? On the kitchen table? In the sink?"

What continued to amaze Art was that Parker paid, and paid well, to get his studly rocks off. Parker, sexual object for hordes of sex-craved kiddy groupies, not to mention the motion-picture wanabees who would do anything for a hand-up, or the legions of star-fuckers and wanna-be-fucked-by-a-star fuckers. All of whom would have paid Parker to feed his big movie-star cock, or any part of it, up their collective asshole.

"I've always been particularly fond of that cougar-skin rug on the floor at the foot of your bed," Art said.

"Can't wait to see you naked on cat skin."

"You think I don't dream nightly about your sexy bod?"

Parker smiled uneasily at the compliment. As good as Parker now looked, whenever stripped bare, his muscles buffed by the rigorous regimen overseen, three times a week, by his personal trainer, he had a tendency not to see the reality of what he'd become but the blubbery someone he'd once been. Parker

simply still couldn't accept that he was frog turned Prince
Charming. More often than not, he felt fat, felt ugly, and felt he
played some horrible trick on everybody who thought him anything other than pitiful Greer Artman.

Somehow, though, whenever he was with Art, Parker never
felt quite as much the fraud he felt when with others.

Art merely figured a guy who had the studly body Parker had
should take every opportunity to flaunt it. In a way, it was
Parker's uncharacteristic modesty, as a movie star, that Art just
might have found the biggest turn-on of all. That and how
Parker had a way of genuinely seeming appreciative for the asshole Art offered him. As if cold cash didn't quite pay for the privilege Parker felt every time Art allowed Parker's big cock thrust
to its big balls up Art's tight ass. Such a hint of appreciation,
whether sincere or merely well-acted, made Art want Parker,
and want Parker's big cock, all the more. So much more that Art
found those needs sometimes downright frightening.

Art was pretty much naked before Parker finally got around
to a slow unbuttoning of his own shirt.

Parker hesitated, his shirt unbuttoned and partially slipped
off one shoulder. He focused on the mirror directly across from
him. Only on very rare occasions did mirrors reflect for Parker
what Parker had become, rather they reflected what he still
imagined he was.

Art walked over to the bed, slid his hands through the breach
of Parker's open shirt and completed the slide of the material off
Parker's studly chest, back, and arms.

"Get up," Art said, as if he'd left the envelope of cash on the
backseat of the limo for Parker, not vice versa.

Art was genuinely relieved and pleased when Parker obliged without resistance.

Cort Forbes

Art went to his knees. With an expertise born of having mastered the complications of many a belt buckle, Art deftly disengaged Parker's horse-head buckle and freed its leather belt. He unbuttoned and unzipped Parker's pants. His hands slid into the waistband of Parker's undershorts, at the hips and, with a push and a slide downward over Parker's firm asscheeks, dropped Parker's pants and briefs.

In coming back to his feet, Art brought his hard cock into contact with Parker's hard cock and slid taut cockbelly against taut cockbelly. Amateurish as he knew it was, Art thought for one full heartbeat that he was going to cream, right then and there.

Art's hands slid Parker's waist and gently coaxed the handsome young movie star to stand even closer. Between them, their naked dicks met in similar sexy embrace. The two pricks might have been clones, so perfectly did they mirror one another. Though the blond hair of one accompanying scrotum, contrasted against the black hair that furred the other, did proclaim the difference, as did how Art's ball-filled sac hung a little lower than the one drooped impressively between Parker's legs.

Art's palms travelled up the exquisite musculature of Parker's back and curled fingertips over Parker's shoulders from back to front.

"Skin so perfect," Art said.

Of all the outrageous things Queer Greer Artman Fartman Fat Boy had suffered, one teenage nemesis from which he'd escaped had been the nightmare Mr. Zits. Even Greer's parents had marvelled as to how their butterball son had suffered only an occasional pimple. At the same time, most of Greer's peers, even the cruelest, despite parents' fortunes spent on dermatologists, had been converted into walking, talking pustules. Greer had merely misconstrued his good fortune as one more punishment from God that make Greer, for one more reason, stand out as different in the crowd.

Art's fingers slid back down the length of Parker's back and over the sexy undulations of Parker's butt.

Art's naked chest moved against Parker's naked chest, Art's nipples hard against Parker's nipples.

Art began a slow return to his knees, without breaking any of the coveted closeness he'd achieved against the young movie star's studly body.

Art kissed Parker's muscled chest as he passed on by. Art's cock slid Parker's right thigh while Parker's dick moved upward along Art's descending belly and chest to the base of Art's neck.

When Art's nose paused to nuzzle Parker's navel, Art pulled Parker's hard cock against the side of Art's face and let Parker's massive boner fuck the space provided between Art's cheek and the palm of Art's hand. As Parker's cockhead slid by, so very close to Art's mouth, Art needed all of his willpower to keep from moving swiftly to cover Parker's cockhead with open lips and, in one mighty swallow, gulp Parker's deliciously naked cock all of the way down to Parker's hair-furred nuts. Few cocks had ever, if ever, tempted Art to risk the usually always potential dangers of AIDS inherent in feasting on any flavorful penile nakedness.

Art made do with a mouthful of Parker's balls, the nuts sucked up one at a time through lips Art pursed purposely small so each nut, when popped through, would experience the pleasure/pain of compression.

"Yes," Parker approved. But then, as far as Parker was concerned, Art could do no wrong. If ever there was a young hustler who seemed able to read Parker's every want and need, that hustler was Art. If ever there was a young man to make Queer

– 91 –

Cort Forbes

Greer Artman Fartman Fat Boy feel completely metamorphosed into studly Parker Crayne, it was Art Monroe.

Art's face leeched to the bottom of Parker's pecker, Art's lips a rubber band that completely encircled Parker's scrotum and held to the exact spot where Parker's sac attached to Parker's cock. Art's nose poked an indentation into the belly of Parker's erect dick.

Art's hands slipped inward, along the crease of Parker's ass, one of Art's fingertips finding Parker's asspucker and giving the spot a slight probe, like a cockhead attempting a dry fuck.

"Stud, stud, stud," Parker chanted. Art and he were positioned so that Parker needed only to turn slightly for the visual tableau the two young men presented within the full-length mirror that veneered one closet door. Parker resisted the temptation to look. He felt too good to risk seeing Art kneeled before Greer Artman's crotch, instead of seeing Art's handsome face having sucked up Parker Crayne's handsome balls.

When finally surrendered, Parker's nuts emerged in a slightly more compact package than when swallowed. The black hair that furred their sac was so heavily saturated with Art's spit that globules of clear saliva beaded the hirsute mesh, like Japanese fishing floats caught in the kelp beds of the Sargasso Sea.

"I'll need two rubbers," Art said, again tempted to make the short detour necessary to swallow Parker's enticingly naked dick, then and there. Parker wouldn't know what hit him until after Art had expertly swallowed Parker's impressive inches all of the way to complete disappearance.

Parker took Art's request for two rubbers as the young hustler's intuitive insight into how Parker, as always, remained thoroughly tempted to sample Art's cock buried to Art's balls up Parker's tight young ass. If Parker, with Art, had discovered the wonders of fucking butt, unknown to Fat Boy Greer Artman, there had been something about Art, and about the hustler's handsome cock, from the very first sighting, that had had Parker tempted to let movie-star asshole ride hustler's impressive erection.

However, any notion Art ever had that he might actually stand a chance of jamming his dick up Parker's studly ass remained nothing more than wildest fantasy. Certainly, it had never formulated to the point where Art would have gone so far as to ask for a condom to carry the fantasy through.

"I suspect it's a helluva lot easier cleaning bed sheets stained with my spilled cum that it will be to clean cougar skin," Art said. Which was his one and only reason for having figured his cock would need a rubber.

"I want your dick naked when I fist it," Parker said. "Don't worry about the cleaning of any dead-cat fur, because it'll be cheap at any cost."

Before getting the rubber for his own dick, however, Parker paused with tantalizing thoughts of what he would do if Art, right then and there, threw caution to the wind and sucked up Parker's naked cock to Parker's balls. Those very thoughts, though, were the final impetus Parker needed to break contact with Art. No longer because he feared what Art might do, but because Parker feared his own decided temptation to let it happen, despite his long-standing fear of AIDS.

Two rolls of condom packets, like rolls of stamps bought at the Post Office for use in a dispenser, only larger, were conveniently just a few steps away, atop a dresser. Parker ripped off one of the packets that contained a lubricated prophylactic.

Art crawled onto the cougar-skin rug. His fingers thrust into the cat's open jaws and anchored among teeth that, while they looked vicious, were no longer even slightly fatal. He lowered his forearms to the rug and aimed his still-elevated ass in Parker's direction.

"Fuck me, stud," Art said. "I've an asshole that's been dying for the feel of your hard dick ever since your cock last tried my butt on for size."

So tempting was the enticement of Art's sexually postured body, Parker's fingers actually trembled as they fumbled open the plastic condom packet and placed the lubricated rubber atop the head of Parker's erect cock. So quickly, in his anxiousness to service Art's asshole, did Parker unroll the latex down Parker's dick, that the young movie star had to make a conscious effort to double-check to make sure the rubber was safely anchored to the shaft of his dick.

"Come on, Parker, fuck me, fuck me," Art said and rolled his ass in blatant, sexual invitation. Nor was his desire for Parker's cock in the least bit faked. He desperately wanted Parker inside of him, wanted the two of them locked sexually together, cockshaft up asshole, belly to butt, chest to back, hand to cock, Parker's fingers latched to Art's bull-like balls.

Parker dropped into the space provided for him between Art's ankles, calves, and knees. He hooked the neck of his dick with his thumb and tugged his cock more to the horizontal. The belly of his rubberized cock whacked against the small of Art's back. Too close to Art's sexy bottom to succeed in actually running rubberized cockhead down the slideway of Art's asscrack, all of the way to Art's asspucker, Parker scooted back a bit, one hand holding to one of Art's hips for support as he did so.

"Take me," Art encouraged. He had become nothing more nor less than a virile young buck in heat. Nothing else suddenly mattered except that his asshole, quick and deep, get speared by Parker's hard, butt-fucking erection.

To offer even farther invitation, Art removed his hands from the cougar's maw and clamped them to his own butt. He yanked his buttcheeks open along their mutually shared crack and fully revealed the oh-so-seemingly-small wink of his anal opening.

So much lust-spawned adrenaline was suddenly loose inside Parker's body that it actually overexcited him to the point where he was less adept, at doing what Art and he both wanted him to do, than he would have been if left more calm, cool, and collected.

"Fuck your studly hustler's ass!" Parker said, his cock taking aim. "Fuck it deep. Fuck it long. Fuck it hard."

"Yeah, you do that for the both of us," Art readily agreed. "'Cause no one wants that any more than I want that, not even you."

Parker doubted there was anyway Art's need for Parker's cock could possibly surpass Parker's need for Art's ass. Parker attributed Art's proclamation to Art's professional acumen that had long ago clued the hustler to the benefits of flattering every paying customer. Who wouldn't be flattered by the illusion that such a handsome young hustler, who'd taken on countless men willing to pay for his services, ass-ridden by all sorts and sizes men and their dicks, could suddenly seem so turned on by one trick, out of so many? Even believing it a lie, Parker found it pleasant to fantasize that Art wasn't faking.

Of all the men Art had ever been with, though, and there had been more than just a few, none did for him what the mere prospect of his asshole having at Parker's big dick did for him. So much did Art want each and every part of Parker's cock fucked inside of him, so much time did Art spend fantasizing just such moments, while he masturbated, or while he entertained paying customers, Art was frightened by it. How many people before him had lost their body and souls to someone who couldn't possibly be theirs? Art was determined, therefore, to take from this relationship what he could. If that meant only a fuck of his ass, now and again by Parker's sexy cock, he was determined to make every fuck from Parker's cock count.

Parker laid his sweaty cheek against Art's sweaty back. Parker banged his sweaty belly against Art's sweaty ass. Parker pounded his condom-sheathed cock up Art's tightly clutching rectum.

It didn't get much better than this, for either young man. Each knew how sublime it was for him, personally, yet doubted any real way the other could be as completely taken in by the sorcery of the moment. Each figured himself in a separate world when, in truth, they were snagged by one and the same whirlwind of passion, of pleasure, and of gut-shattering ecstasy.

They had fucked enough times to be acutely familiar with each other and, therefore, progressed faster toward orgasm than they had during their initial, more exploratory, fucks. Which had the advantage of skipping most of the fumbles that generally might have interrupted pleasure flows, though it had the disadvantage of shrinking the time they needed together.

It may have resembled a rough and woolly ride, Parker's cock up Art's asshole, but it was the end result of trial and error that had finally honed the fuck into choreographed performance, of two perfectly matched sexual dancers, that it had become.

"Yes, oh, yes, oh ... oh!" Art said and gave his butt yet another slight roll that stirred Parker's fucking cock deep inside him.

Parker focused what little attention he could muster into coordinating his beating of Art's cock to coincide with Parker's onrush to orgasm.

Beating cock wasn't beating cock wasn't beating cock, in that every cock had a life all its own, a distinct personality, a way of indicating where it was in the Grand Opera of any fuck. If all the signs provided by a cock were read properly, whomever whipped that dick toward climax could pretty well tell the where and the when of it. Art's cock enlarged within Parker's pumping fist. Art's cockshaft veins became more prominent against Parker's palm. A slight wetness suddenly appeared within Art's cockmouth and was transferred from there, and spread along the length of Art's burgeoning erection, by Parker's pumping fingers.

Art's scrotum went prune-like and hugged Art's testicles tightly to the base of Art's hard cock. No amount of Parker's kneading of Art's nuts softened the ever-growing toughness of those nuts' scrotal shell. However, the balls did become more and more noticeably large as they were required to hold more and more cum prior to blast-off.

Parker's balls no longer slapped Art's ass whenever an inslide of Parker's hard-on ended with a collision of Parker's belly against Art's ass. Anyone who wanted to talk nuts that were ballooned to capacity, by newly manufactured cum, would have had to include Parker's testicles in the conversation. Parker's gonads were giant-size in his scrotum. They were so full of cream that they strained at their each and every seam, their floodgates kept locked only by Parker's sheer determination to have Art and Parker's climaxes coincide.

"Fuck me!" Art bellowed to the bedroom walls.

Parker, his nuts finally unable to contain their mess of reservoired cum any longer, caught a glimpse of himself in the mirror, Parker so obviously riding Art's sexy ass. Parker was genuinely surprised not to see Queer Greer Artman Fartman Fat Boy hunched over Art's attractive and studly body. Nor did Queer Greer Artman Fartman Fat Boy appear throughout the whole cataclysmic upheaval that shook both handsome young men senseless and left them, at the end of their ride, cum-drained and seemingly rolled through a wringer for deposit quite bone-less, not to mention boner-less, on the other side.

Later that evening, Art was possessed of a sudden urge to come right on out and say — Come on, Parker, how about I pack up my things and move right in here with you? We obviously hit it off together. I have a better time with you than I've ever had with anyone. Hell, I spend all my time, not with you, just think-ing about you. It's not just the good sex, either. I've had good sex with other people. Obviously, it's something way above and beyond the sex. It's: I like you. Hell, it's: I may even love you. You're admittedly a good actor, but I think I'd know if you didn't actually mean it every time you tell me I'm the best ever for you, too. Whatever there is between us, it's not something that hap-pens between two people all that often. So, we should explore its potential. Not just by having me check in, now and again for the occasional screw, but by having me around on a permanent basis.

What Art did say was: "Try not being such a stranger between now and the next time." After all, Parker was a god-damned movie star who had his pick of just about every hand-some guy in the movies and out. What in the hell would he want permanently with Art who was just an everyday kind of sell-his-cock-and-ass hustler from the meat racks of Boyland Park?

Parker was tempted, right then and there, to ask the hand-some hustler to move in with him. With Art, Parker felt more alive than he ever felt with anyone else. Art even seemed to keep the ghost of Queer Greer Artman Fartman Fat Boy at bay.

Parker desperately needed someone to talk with, confide in, care for, love. He needed an occasional safe haven in this hurricane movie-star existence into which he'd so unexpectedly been thrust as Parker Crayne. Parker felt lost at sea a good deal of the time. His time spent with Art was not only sexually satisfying but calming, in comparison with what the rest of his life had become.

"Here, I've something for you," is what Parker did say. He went to the nearby dresser and retrieved a money-stuffed envelope from the top drawer. "A little something extra, by way of special thank-you." After all, how long would any relationship last between Parker and a handsome hustler who had his pick and choose of countless handsome young men, especially once Art discovered that Parker wasn't really Parker Crayne but pathetic little butterball Greer Artman? Greer only temporarily able to pull the wool over everyone's eyes?

From his penthouse window, Parker watched the limo, Art inside, exit the driveway and turn left into the residential street.

Parker went into his bedroom and laid on the bed.

Across from him, evident within the mirror that veneered one closet door, although Parker didn't bother to look, knowing what was there, was the reflected image of Queer Greer Artman Fartman Fat Boy curled into a fetal position atop the covers of the bed.

PLAY IT AGAIN, SAM

Tuesday, July 6, 11:59 p.m.:

The youth's trousers bulged his crotch, the thickness of his cock well-evident where it crawled almost obscenely along his left thigh. He took a firmer stance against the tree, spread his legs and assumed an even more provocative pose. He wore a T-shirt, the cloth of which stretched tightly across his well-muscled chest, his nipples pressed visibly through the white cotton. His well-tanned arms, swollen by nicely sculptured biceps and triceps, stretched short sleeves almost to ripping. He smiled invitingly. His teeth were white, even in the darkness. His eyes, their color indistinguishable in the shadows, were partially shielded by the abundance of his lush blond hair.

Sam, as young or even younger, clearly as blond as the muscled youth, but not nearly as well-muscled, walked by him and gave no invitation he wanted to be followed. Sam didn't even return the muscled blond's smile.

Like a firefly, the hot tip of a cigarette blazed its small coal in the distance. It smouldered brighter as the thin Negro drew its invisible smoke into his lungs. Sam tried to circumvent the Negro, but the black moved to intercept.

"Could you tell me the time?" the black asked. He was middle-aged, his features soft, delicate, almost feminine.

Sam smiled at the complete unoriginality of the question. But then, what else could one ask: Want to fuck? Want to suck?

Those were more to the point, but were the exceptions, except when dealing with the hustlers who frequented the other end of the park.

"It's just after midnight," Sam said. His smile faded. He didn't want the Negro to think Sam gave any encouragement. Even under ordinary circumstances, Sam preferred his tricks butch and with white meat.

"I guess it's way past park closing," the Negro made one more attempt.

"Yes," Sam verified and moved into the shadows.

The Negro, left uncertain, stood for an instant and tried to decide whether Sam's smile had offered invitation. He decided it hadn't, and he turned to hopefully greener pastures in the opposite direction.

Two boys talked on the steps of the park gazebo. Suspiciously, they eyed Sam headed their way. Sam detoured to the left of them and disappeared into shrubbery. On the gazebo, one youth pulled his swollen cock from his open fly. The other youth dropped to his knees, lowered his head, and swallowed the offered turgid shaft of steel-hard meat.

The number of people cruising thinned as Sam approached the most densely wooded segment of the park. This particular area, a popular meeting place for homosexuals during the day, pretty much emptied by twilight. In that, there was no man-made lighting to dilute its eery darkness. Only the moon occasionally managed to piss a few streamers of yellow through interlocking leaves and branches.

No bodies leaned against trees, no legs spread wide, no thick pricks hand-pressed to larger outlines beneath trouser flies. No cigarette tips flared to greater brightness by sucking mouths. No young men talked or made love among the brush.

No requests were made for the time of night, for a smoke, or for directions.

The hand came from behind, clamped tightly over Sam's mouth and nose. Another hand and arm reached around Sam's mid-section, pulled the young man's body back into a solid mass of manly, naked muscle. The arm about Sam's belly took his breath away. The hand over his nose and mouth prevented him from getting air. For an instant, Sam thought he would suffocate.

Sam was thrown to the ground. His whole body reverberated from the fall. A man's hunky body fell on top of him. Sam failed in all attempts to push the man off. The man's darkness-blurred face, part of the dimly smothering mass, came close to Sam's face and pushed firm lips roughly against Sam's lips. The man's thick tongue pushed far down Sam's throat.

Sam felt the strength of all the man's naked muscle devoted to the task of keeping Sam pinned tightly to the ground.

Sam tried to cry out, but his assailant's lips kept pressed against Sam's own. Each noise Sam uttered became lost within the other's steamy, humid mouth.

The man's hard and naked lower body clamped its legs to the outside of Sam's legs. Naked man-cock pressed against Sam's hard cock, man-prick and youth-prick separated only by the cloth of Sam's jeans. Sam's hands ran hard and naked man-flesh, over the ropy muscles of naked man-back to the swells of rock-solid naked man-butt.

"Take it easy, and you won't get hurt," the naked and sexually aroused man said. His voice was low and guttural. "Just relax."

Sam tried to roll from under the man's weight, but the chore proved impossible.

"What do you want?" Sam asked

"I want you to relax!" the man said.

The man's hand hooked Sam's shirt, at its neck, and ripped the cloth away. Hard warm man-flesh now covered Sam's naked chest. Manly nipples met Sam's youthful nipples. All four nipples were hard as small ball bearings.

Sam was at a physical disadvantage. He knew that now, just as he'd known it from the very beginning, when ham-like man-hands clamped over his mouth, when the immense weight of man-muscled flesh and bone pressed down upon him.

"Oh, yes!" the man said and his hands claimed those of the youth to force the latter to Sam's sides. "You're only going to make it better for me by struggling."

Sam tried, yet again, to pull his hands free, tried, yet again, to roll free of the man's vise-like press.

"Please," Sam said, his struggles still to no avail.

"Please, what?" the man asked, his voice filled with the confidence of his obviously superior power. "Please fuck you?"

The man pushed to a sitting position, astride Sam's thighs. Large man-hands fumbled with the crotch buttons of Sam's pants.

"No!" Sam said, sat up, and closed his hands around the man's thick throat. The man's neck tendons bulged beneath Sam's grip. Sam's hands were unable to close around so massive a handful.

Almost too easily, the man pulled Sam's hands free, pushed Sam back to the ground. Suddenly lifting himself on his knees, the man expertly rolled Sam within the space between the man's commanding kneel.

Hardly knowing how it was done, Sam found himself flipped to his belly. Equally surprising, the man oh-so-easily yanked down Sam's pants but kept the youth completely under control.

With Sam's ass vulnerable and bare, the man collapsed along Sam's back, and the head of the man's thick cock, like a missile aimed at a specific heat source, oh so quickly found its target, which was Sam's pucker, and force-fed cockhead and cockneck fast and furious into the depth of Sam's protesting asshole.

The man's legs parenthesized the youth's legs and hugged them. The man's lower belly pushed hard into Sam's ass and ground hard cock up tight asshole. The man's balls banged frantically against the Sam's balls. The man's chest laid hard and tight against Sam's back.

"Please," Sam pleaded.

"Sure, kid. No need to beg. I'll gladly fuck the shit out of you."

Sam grunted as the man's cock pulled out, almost to its bulbous head, then plunged right back in again . Sam grunted again as the same thick cock once again withdrew almost entirely from the boy's spasming hole, only once again to drive all of the way in. Sam's asshole seemed destined to rip, beneath the size and force of the cock's attack.

The tube-like hunk of man-cock slipped out, then jammed in — out, in, out, in — all the while it prodded Sam's prostate like a billy club prodded a helpless vagrant.

Sam's cock pulsed its own steely hardness between the ground and the youth's belly.

"Tight!" the man's voice breathed in Sam's ear. "My God, but you've got one hell of a tight stinkhole. And, it's chewing, chewing, chewing up my goddamned cock."

"Please," Sam moaned.

Sam's continued pleas only pushed his assailant to greater

speeds. Fuck strokes became shorter and more powerful. The man's hipbones bruised the youth's crotch-slapped ass.

"You like getting fucked in your ass," the man panted in Sam's ear, and it wasn't a question. "You like getting it from a real man. He-man prick pushed in and pulled out of that rear end of yours? Big male cock stuffed so far and so deep up your guts that you feel it in the bottom of your throat. My blasted wad going to blow right on out the other end of your mouth, like great wads of white water geysered from Old Faithful."

On cue, the man's cock swelled even bigger. Its additional size caused additional friction from each and every pump within hugging asshole walls. The more the friction, the more the exquisite pleasure/pain that sunburst from Sam's molested asshole to the rest of the youth's body.

Sam pressed his face into the hard ground. Mashed and moist leaves clung to his cheek. He moaned and felt bits of dirt on his wet lips and tongue. He smelled the pungency of damp earth.

"You're the best ass I've ever fucked, kid," the man said and caught his breath.. Finally, he managed: "You're giving this old whanger of mine a royal workout. My old balls just dying to spray and baste hot white slime up your tightly clutching hole."

The man's hips gained additional momentum. His thick prick was an up-and-down pile driver gone wild within Sam's butt.

"Agghhhh!" the man groaned. His body spasmed on top of Sam. His belly ground frantically into the youth's ass. His hot sperm jettisoned sperm from his huge submerged cock. Thick and coagulated juices oozed along the sides of the man's plugged-to-its-roots penis.

Sam lie motionless, as temporarily drained as the man collapsed atop him. Finally, the man rolled off, and his softening prick slipped out of Sam's asshole, an inch at a time, with a suctioning sound of foot and leg out of muck that pulled a flood of stale jism with it. The man's large and heart-shaped cockhead was the last to exit the buttocks and did so with a decided champagne-cork "Pop!"

The man's whole, now drooping, fourteen inches of cock were wet and shiny with slime.

The man got to his feet, and his muscular body glistened with the sweat of his orgasm. His black hair banged his eyes. His massive cock and balls now hung to his knees. He looked at the Sam's just-fucked body which was white within the shadows of the night. The man turned and walked into the woods.

Sam lie quiet and listened to the sounds of moving branches and leaves as his assailant disappeared farther into the darkness. Finally, even those sounds were gone.

Sam got to his feet, his belly and thighs covered with dirt and with the mess of his own spermal discharge.

He found his pants, thrown carelessly over a nearby shrub. The branches of the squat bush were squashed, having been pressed beneath the weight of Sam's denim, like Sam had been pressed beneath the body of the man who'd fucked him. Sam pulled his pants on over his sweaty body and zipped up his pants crotch over his spent penis.

Tuesday, July 27, 11:57 p.m.:

The thick prick was evident through the sand-papered thinness of the young man's jeans. It snaked thickly down his left thigh. The globes of the young man's balls and the bullet-like shape of the young man's circumcised cockhead were easily delineated within the stretched denim. The young man wore a black T-shirt. His muscular pectorals bulged the cloth. His hair was blond and looked windblown in the shadows. He was joined by another youth, dark-haired and thin. The two talked for a few minutes, then moved off into the shadows together in search of an even more secluded spot.

Sam detoured around them and walked toward the gorge on the other side of a dark copse of trees.

There were two studs who stood on the bridge that spanned the gorge. Each eyed Sam invitingly and, without words, asked the inevitable question. The blond dropped his hand sensuously to his bulged groin and caressed the grapefruit mound of his genitalia that strained his pants crotch to bursting.

Sam didn't meet either's gaze. He didn't want to give either any encouragement.

Sam looked at his watch. The illuminated dials read a little after midnight.

Sam took the path that snaked down the side of the gully. He glanced furtively behind to insure that he wasn't followed. Few people ventured into the gully after dark. Too many people had been robbed there, beaten up there, or had even worse happen to them in the gully's darkness. Above Sam, the dark underside of the steel and cement bridge shut out all light.

No bodies stood by the sides of the path. No one spread his legs, pressed his thick prick to even larger bulge within a cushioning nest of pubic hair thick-grown between pants-tented legs. No lighted cigarette was moved in the darkness by a nervous hand. No one asked the time of night, or for a smoke, or for directions.

The hand came from behind, clamped tightly over Sam's mouth and nose. Another hand and arm reached around Sam's mid-section, pulled the young man's body back into a solid mass of manly, naked muscle. The arm about Sam's belly...

POET-VOYEUR

Once within an evening's darkness,
I detoured through Boyland Park, lest
I had to walk the distance all around.
In that this city's planned wilderness,
With paths and landscape, most quite lightless,
Were between my apartment and the town.

I'll confess another reason
Was how the warmth of the season
Drew others, besides me, into that spot.
Where hills and gullies, also, the gloom,
Provided us with sufficient room
To do what we had come to do — a lot.

For if our needs weren't quite the same,
No doubts we played similar games.
Each game which had, smack at its central core,
Our search for like-minded men and sex.
Of which success was a nightly test
To see whom could rack the far better score.

Cort Forbes

At first, some stud made the mistake,
Thinking me there to eat his steak
And fished his steely monster from his pants.
It was mighty big and ham-like thick;
Obviously more than twelve-inch prick.
I wasn't there to do that kind of dance.

I said, "No thanks, but call me back,
If you should ever find asscrack
That's willing to accept this daunting task:
Your cock thrust so deeply in its hole
That the butt risks ripping on your pole.
Especially if you make that fucking last."

A second stud, mistaken, too,
Dropped his pants to show me the view
Of firm and pliant asscheeks and his back.
He opened buns along sweaty crease,
Upon his pucker let my eyes feast,
And asked if I would probe his tight young crack.

I could see the potential there:
The sexy sight of his ass, bare,
Inviting stuffing of some prick inside.
If he could find some other's large nuts,
Some other's hard cock thrust in his guts,
I'd be so pleased to watch his ass oblige.

Poet Voyeur

But the way things were, then and there,
In order that I be quite fair,
As far as pleasures which I did require,
I had to decline whomever's ass,
As I'd rejected cock, shortly past.
I needed something more to light my fire.

I saw a black I'd seen before,
Who fucked so well men begged for more.
He had in tow a shirtless blond young man.
The latter's denim crotch, sanded thin,
Little hid the stiffened cock within,
The girth of which too big for any hand.

I followed them until they stopped,
And the shirtless blond's pants were dropped
To form a sexy puddle 'round his feet.
His naked ass, a firm sight to see,
Or so I thought from behind my tree.
Exciting, too, the jutting of his meat.

Likewise, I was immensely awed
By the black man's hard cock when pawed
From out the breach of that man's opened fly.
Black scooping fingers did scarce control
How ebon, fist-sized, gonads both did roll
To freedom I was oh-so-quick to spy.

Cort Forbes

The blond bowed deeply, from his waist.
The black stepped in with calm, not haste,
And latex was unrolled o'er big black dick.
Then holding open the blond's rear end,
Black knelt behind what he'd soon be in,
Stuck out his tongue and gave a hearty lick.

My cock was out and in my hand.
My meat was hot as any brand.
I stroked my hefty handful, down, up, down.
I watched the black man, still on his knees,
And gave my cum-filled gonads a squeeze
For sticky juice with which to slick cockcrown.

The blond's asscrack, now drenched with spit,
The black man gave that ass a whip
And then got up, no longer on his knees.
Then, he positioned black cockhead, large,
To the blond's pucker, black man in charge,
And slipped black cock in, easy as you please.

"Fuck me!" bellowed the cock-stuck stud.
The black man reached for blond kid's pud,
And, likewise, reached a hand for blond kid's nuts.
Black man's hand made cum-filled worlds collide,
As all the while, black cock fucked inside,
Pumping, pumping, pumping the young man's guts.

Poet Voyeur

"I'll fuck you good," the black man said.
"Make your blond asshole nice and red.
My dick lodged really deep up your behind.
Your prostate feeling my big cock's touch,
And once my hot load of cum is gushed,
You'll think your insides basted mighty fine.

"Oh, yes!" the blond kid's throaty gasp.
"I love your black cock up my ass.
You fuck me, and I only beg for more.
So, beat my cock and squeeze my gonads,
Because I'm better than all the lads
Who've ever played at black man's whore before."

I was getting hot and sweaty,
Cock and balls poised at the ready,
As I watched and skillfully flogged my hog.
My hairy scrotum was compacted
Against my cockbase where contacted
My penis large and hard as any log.

Proclaimed the black: "I'm real close, kid.
My balls about to pop their lids."
Black snuggled closer yet to white kid's back.
Black belly hit blond ass and locked there,
Uniting pubic black and blond hair,
As found on black man's crotch and blond kid's crack.

The cum from blond's big dick, it fanned
In mighty squirts that webbed black hand.
At just which time my ballooned nuts let go.
I shot my cum, heavy, hard and fast,
While my fingers squeezed to make it last,
Until none of us had more cum to blow.

The black man's rubbered dick came out.
Pearly cum ballooned rubber snout.
The black man threw used latex to one side.
The blond pulled up his discarded jeans,
His bare ass and cock no longer seen.
Then, my spent cock I did proceed to hide.

I turned away, my interest gone,
Once my hot cum had splattered lawn.
But shortly down a nearby wooded path,
I chanced on two sex-linked, studly men,
The sight of whom swelled my cock again,
And held more promise for a night not past.

WHEN OPPORTUNITY KNOCKS

I take his money and pocket it.

Unknown to him, though, I'm not going to fuck him just because of the money. I like his looks. More than that, though, I just like sex. I used to give sex away, only came to this side of Boyland Park a couple of months ago to see what it was like. I was just going to shoot on through and play voyeur, see what was going for dollars while the rest of us indulged ourselves for free. Truthfully, I wasn't all that impressed by what I saw, although it turned out to be just an off-night. Saw a couple of guys, both so ugly I couldn't believe either one was getting paid. Maybe it was the top man's big cock that was the cause for an exchange of dollars. Surprising just how many guys willingly come up with hard cash for an enormously hard wanker. I need more than just a big cock to turn me on, even if I were paying. Which is why I earlier, this very night, turned down the guy who said his name was Lad. There was just something about Lad — maybe the way he looked at me disconcertingly cross-eyed? — that just didn't do it for me. Maybe the way his name came across as that of a dog.

Niles, now, he's okay.

Of course, his name isn't any more likely Niles than my name is really Bart. You just need something to call a guy, don't you? I mean, how's it sound ... "Fuck me, whomever-you-may-be!"?

Cort Forbes

"Can I see a bit more than just your cock and balls before you fuck my ass?" Niles asks. "You look like you've a good body."

"What exactly do you have in mind, Niles?" I say. "I'm not keen on getting stark naked. Although police raids are blessedly far and few between, I don't want sex too complicated if I have to head on out in a hurry."

"Your chest," he says. "I'd like to see that. Your belly, too. You've got a washboarded belly, I'd bet money on it."

"You want me to unbutton my shirt. I can do that." There's an old Meat Loaf song about doing anything for love. Except, is this love? Too fun, I think, for love. Everyone I know who's in love, or been there, has pretty much ruined fun sex with all sorts of complicated emotional baggage.

"You must work out with weights," Niles says. Unbuttoned, my shirt reveals a nice slice of my pectorals, plus pectoral cleavage, plus ridged abdominals, plus knotted navel.

"Yeah, I work out," I say. It's a lie, though. Whatever I've got, I've got because of genes. My dad's built like a brick shithouse and never worked out a day in his life. His success in sports kept his muscle definition honed. I suppose, my success in sports hones my muscles, too. Maybe that's what I should have said. Except, Niles probably isn't really interested. He just makes conversation. I enjoy sex more where there's not quite so much chit-chat. Although, there's less of it on this side of the park. On the other side of the park, people seem to think free sex means you're actually on some kind of a date that requires small talk as an integral part of seduction.

"Can I touch?" Niles asked. "Your stomach, I mean."

"Sure you wouldn't like to touch my cock?" My hard-on is thrust through my unzipped pants. I don't wear underwear, not even after having once been offered a hundred bucks by some really horny guy who wanted to take a pair of my shorts home to snarf at leisure.

"The only place I want that cock of yours is up my ass, and we'll have that happen soon now," he says. He slips both his hands through the breached material of my shirt. He places his palms flat over my nipples. His hands are slightly callused and make me wonder what he does for a living. I had him pegged as a doctor, a lawyer, or some other white-collar professional. Obviously, I was wrong. Although, he does have impeccably clean fingernails.

"You want to rubberize my dick, or do you want me to do it?" I know one guy who creams just unrolling condom latex along the length of my up-jutted penis.

"I suppose you can't be talked out of the rubber, huh?" He may think he just sounds hopeful. To me, he sounds downright suicidal.

"I don't do anything without veiling the old monkey." There has never a day I fucked my naked cock up naked butt. I missed out completely on all those years of all-sex-is-safe-sex promiscuity about which some old-timers talk about as nostalgically as Christians talk about the missing holy grail.

"I've a lubricated condom," he says. He leaves one hand over one of my nipples. Both my nipples are hard as tacks. "You put it on while I watch."

"You into watching, Niles? That your bag?"

"I'm into fucking," he says. "You're going to be surprised at how a guy so into fucking as I am comes to you with such a tight asshole tucked within the crease of my ass."

What will really surprise me is if he's right. I've had guys brag about their tight asses when I would have had to have had a cock the size of a rocket to get anywhere near a tight fit.

I take the offered rubber and check, diplomatically as possible, to make sure the packaging isn't tampered with. I've heard of guys pinpricking rubbers so that the condoms will rip and come free once lodged up some butthole — just for the joy of unrubberized cock fucking their rectums. It boggles my mind to hear of people willing to take such unwarranted risks. It's not as if there isn't more than enough pleasure to be had from a raincoated dick.

Both Niles' hands are back on my chest. His fingers slide along my sides, until only the pads of his thumbs remain hatted on my nipples. When he slides his hands farther, his thumbs leave the centers of my teats all the harder and standing tall.

"Nice, nice body," he says.

"You want to shed some of your clothes, too?"

"Naw. I wouldn't want you turned off by a body less perfect than yours."

He looks pretty damned good in what he's wearing. Maybe there's just the slightest hint that he's carrying around a bit more weight than the doctor ordered, but I've always preferred a bit of meat on my tricks' bones, as compared to downright skeletal. Some athletes on the verge of going to seed, my father a case in point, have some of the sexiest bodies I've ever seen.

"Okay by me," I say. It's his money paid, after all, and I've never come cheap, at least on this side of the park. When in Rome, do as the Romans.

"Think we can unbuckle your belt?" he asks.

"You mean, do I really want my pants tumbled to my ankles." I've one end ripped off the condom packet. Some of the inside lubricant soaks my fingers.

"I'd really like to see your pants around your feet," he says.

"Maybe if you unfasten the top button of my trousers, too?" I suggest, deciding to be magnanimous when just the unbuckling of my belt doesn't quite do the trick.

He unfastens the button, and my pants drop.

"Speaking of dropped pants, it's going to be kind of hard to fuck your ass with your pants still on, Niles. Unless you've got a strategically placed rip within the buttcrack of your trousers."

"How'd you guess?" He thinks I'm psychic. Actually, I'd been joking. Who could know?

"You want this cock of mine, Niles?" We've about exhausted our limited repertoire of small-talk. He might not be ready for sex, but I am.

"Yeah, I want it, Bart," he says.

He turns. He bends over, his ass aimed in my direction. The opening in the asscrack of his trousers reveals the opening in the asscrack of his butt. He's no more wearing underpants than I am. His pucker becomes more evident when he man-handles his buttcheeks and pulls already breached pants material even wider.

"I'm ready," he says. "I've one mighty cock-hungry asshole ready, too. How many inches of cock you got there, Bart? Nine inches if you've got a one, right?"

"Maybe a slight exaggeration on your part," I say.

"But not much of one." It's not a question. He's had enough dick up his butt to pretty well judge the size of whatever the hard-on headed in his asshole's direction.

I'm always surprised when anyone insinuates my nine inches are big. Then again, that's possibly because I've seen more than my share of big cocks in my time, and apparently missed all those supposedly average-size six-inch pricks out there somewhere. I wonder what size cock Niles has. His crotch remains nicely filled with something. Cock and balls? Stuffed sock from his stocking drawer? Maybe he's just shy. Surprisingly, or maybe not, a lot of people are uptight about their bodies. Niles certainly wasn't shy about offering cash for sex and in getting me stripped just the way he wants me.

"Cock incoming," I tell him.

I've waited for some of the lubricant on the rubber to evaporate, but I have second thoughts as his pucker looks smaller and smaller. Could it really be as snug as he promises?

I step in, simultaneously hooking my dick with the thumb of my right hand to weigh down my stiffy to a horizontal, as opposed to its naturally erect vertical, position.

I mash the nippled tip of my condom between my cockhead and his pucker. That his sphincter doesn't immediately roll open, despite the pressure already applied to the entrance to his asshole, is a very good sign. Another good sign is the way, when his butt does begin to roll open, like the eye of a camera, it's suddenly a rubber band snugly vise-like around the head of my dick.

"Does seem yours is a snug little bunghole," I say and hold his hips so I don't tumble him over on his head as I feed him a good three inches of my stiff dick.

"God, I do love hefty meat up my ass," he says and provides a back-buck of his butt that impales his asshole on yet another three inches of my prick. "When it's hefty and young, like yours is hefty and young, all the better."

He's never asked my age, although some guys do. I look younger than I am. Some guys only give me an oh-yeah grin when I assure them that I'm of legal age. Very few, though, decide to pass me up once I make myself available, even if they're convinced I'm lying. Hell, I can't be all that young with all the hair sprouted at the roots of my pecker. Maybe they only ask my age because they think I'm a cop out to entrap them.

"Uggghhhh!" I say. His tight asshole — and, yes, it is as tight as promised — has contracted around all of my cock that I've so far managed to get inside it. That part of my dick in his ass actually seems squeezed to half again its normal circumference and to twice again its normal length, up his rectum.

For some cockamamie reason, I figure that I'll stretch his asshole a bit by feeding him what remains of my erection. When all that feeding accomplishes is my total inches finally up his still-tight butt, my bare belly flush against the butt of his trousers, every bit of my cock strangled to within an inch of its life. As if Niles' asshole is an anaconda, and my cock is some smaller snake of which the bigger vigorously makes a meal.

I kind of hunch my upper body over his, still holding to his hips for support.

"You want me to fist your cock, or anything?" I ask. I'm not so long from the free side of the park that I don't at least make the offer, now and again, to provide a bit of reciprocity. Especially if the guy is nice and not pushy. Some guys, if they want jacked off while I fuck them, have to pay extra or flog their own hog.

"You just fuck my ass, stud," Niles says. "My cock'll take care of itself."

I can't do more than ask. I do wonder if I've one of those guys who can cream with just the feel of something — preferably hard cock — fucked up their assholes. Spontaneous orgasm has never happened to me, but the only thing I've let up my butt is my finger. Not that I haven't, at times, been more than prepared to offer my ass to some guy, only to discover he, and most guys like him, seem to expect me, a paid hustler, always to play top man. So often has that occurred, as a matter of fact, that I'm not bragging when I say I've become more than a little proficient in that particular role. One of these days, though, I'll lose my butch good looks, certainly lose my youth, and then I can possibly explore the possibilities of creaming with just the feel of some guys dick working, working, working, my rectum, instead of vice versa.

Since Niles, for whatever his reasons, isn't offering up his cock or his balls for me to play with, I leave my hands anchored on his hips, my fingers locked over his hipbones.

"Pump me, Bart," he says, apparently anxious for my cock to do a bit more than just remain plugged to its fullest up his rear end. "Don't worry about hurting me. I've asshole lined with steel."

His asshole certainly feels, more and more, like a steel trap. I suddenly wonder if I'm going to be able to give this bastard his monies' worth. Fucking his butt is like trying to pass a camel, back and forth, back and forth, through the eye of a needle. Each time I get my dick out as far as my cockhead, his gumming sphincter manages to hold so firmly to whatever loose skin sheathes my hard inner cockcore that my prick suddenly has even more of a foreskin than it ever did before my prepuce was clipped.

"Yes ... yes," he says as I plug my dick back up his backside. My scrotum keeps swinging, after my belly hits his ass, and my nuts whack against the overhanging trouser seat of his britches.

Not that my balls will swing nearly as free in just a few short seconds. Already my scrotum does its compaction that will eventually hoist my testicles securely to the base of my dick.

"Oh, yes," he says.

"I'm glad his asshole has lost just a bit of its original tightness. Not that it still isn't as snug as a rubber glove. In fact, I purposely concentrate on pinpointing the whereabouts of my condom up his butt for fear that the existing friction has already disrobed my dick and made it, as well as Niles' asshole, suddenly vulnerable to only God knows what. Luckily, a quick glance between my belly and Niles' ass, on an out-pull of my cockinches from Niles' butt, shows my condom having ridden only half an inch up my cockshaft from its original snug fit about the base of my erection.

I take the few seconds it requires, on the next complete slides of my cock up Niles' butt, to use a thumb and forefinger to press the open end of my rubber more fully down around my cockbase.

I'm glad my cock isn't one of those leakers that can be sexier than hell but juice up the insides of a rubber so much, prior to a real cum, that they're forever in more danger of slipping free of their raincoat than my dry cock ever is. Before AIDS, leaky dicks were all the rage, because they supplied their own natural lubricant. Now, since a guy usually wears a pre-lubricated rubber, or at least greases down an unlubricated one, unless both partners are into the pleasure/pain of a dry fuck, weepy dicks aren't nearly as advantageous as they once were.

As a matter of fact, my dry dick, encased within its slime-coated rubber, is doing a damned good job up Niles' asshole.

"Doing a real good job," I confirm and don't make it a question. "My cock up your ass," I add, in case he doesn't get the gist.

"Yeah, stud," Niles agrees. "Make it even better. Make it even faster. Make it even harder. Make it even deeper."

My obliging him with three out of four isn't bad. As for the "even deeper", I'm afraid a just-short-of-nine-inch cock doesn't manage any deeper than those just-under-nine inches. Niles knew what he was getting when he bought the package. Had he thought my dick too small, he would likely have said so.

"Feels good. Feels real good," he assures me that he's not really complaining.

I roll my hips a couple of times on both an in- and an out-slide. If I can't get my cock pushed any deeper than it present-ly goes, I can fuck his butt from varying angles.

"Oh, Jesus, yes!" He's appreciative. "Collide your big dick one more time with my prostate."

I guess the where and when, and my dick hits his walnut-size gland and proceeds right on by.

I'm really holding on to Niles by now. No longer because I'm fearful of toppling him forward on his head, but because I'm real-ly getting carried away on the wings of the screw. I want to make sure I keep my balance. I'm supposed to be the professional here, although I'm really less a professional than Niles probably figures. It will look damned amateurish, even to me, if I fuck us both into a nose-dive.

I prefer a wider stance, but my feet are pretty much tied up by my trousers dropped around my ankles. I'm wearing boots that can't be easily removed or stepped out of, so I make do with the stance I've got.

My pants dropped, my shirt open, my crotch and chest belly bare, I transfer a lot of my sweat to the seat of Niles' pants. Except, I can't tell how much, because his pants are a really dark shade of black. Probably on purpose. Any guy who has a hole ready-made in the crack of his trouser ass, and who doesn't wear underpants, certainly has the same forethought to choose the proper color for his night on the town. That is if black is a color; I've always been a little confused about that, as well as where white fits into any picture. Not that I give either black or white that much concentration at the moment.

"How's it coming, Niles?" I've got his money in my pocket, and there are hustlers who, after they've got the cash, figure all else they have to do is blast their cream into the rubbers stuffed up their customers' asses. I'm still naive enough, though, to want to give any customer of mine his sense of money well-spent. The only trouble with a guy like Niles, who doesn't pro-duce his dick for me to get hold of and better estimate when and if it's close to climax, is that I'm reduced to playing it entirely by ear. "Want to tell me just where you are, in the general scheme of things?" I ask for in-put.

Well-paid or not, I'm not going to fuck an asshole this tight, hell probably not even fuck one loose as a goose, for all damned night. Already my nuts are pretty well grouped tightly against the base of my dick. Already, I've this pleasurable feeling in the pit of my belly that tells me it's not going to take that many more pushes and pulls, of my dick up Niles' asshole, before all of my pleasure funnels right to my balls and squirts, via my butt-filling erection, to balloon the rubber I'm slipping and sliding within Niles' rear end.

"You've got me really primed, man," Niles says. "You've got the cum in my nuts squealing to be let free."

I hope he's right, because I give him an even harder and a faster fuck. Not because he asks for it, not because I con-sciously make the concerted effort, but because there's no help-ing myself. My cock delivers its rabbit-like punches, the resounding whump, whump, whump, of my belly and crotch against his cloth-covered ass, because my fucking is no longer under the control of my brain. I can't stop screwing Niles now, even if one or the other of us should suddenly want me to.

Cort Forbes

Not that either of us is hot to have me stop.

"Yes ... yes ... fuck ... fuck ... my ... ass. Fuck my ass. Fuckmyassssss!"

I really sock it to him, like a boxer's fist hits a punching bag. Bang ... bang ... bang ... bang.   Is that where they get the term "banging" a guy's asshole?

"I'm going to cream," Niles says, but it should have been me saying it, because it's my nuts letting go.

"Aaaghhhh ... aghhh ... aghhhhhhurghhh!" All I can manage at the moment. I tend to get pretty speechless at moments like this. I can be a Chatty Cathy, right up to orgasm, but when my cum lets to, I pretty much revert to the primitive. Suddenly, I'm one of those cavemen whose vocal cords never quite evolved enough for intelligent speech. I just grunt all over the damned place.

"Fill my butt with cock and cum!" Nick makes it all more clear than anything I've been able to come up with. He must find what he says a turn on, too, because he turns it into some kind of Gregorian chant: "Cock and cum ... cock and cum ... cock and cummmmmmmmmmm ..."

I fed him all of the cock I've got, in one final lunge, and I leave my dick stuffed up his behind from my cockhead to my balls. For extra measure, suddenly out to feed him whatever part of my dick might be hiding beneath my belly, I grind my stomach tighter into his butt. I lift up on my toes, and more of my spunk blasts from my dick into the ballooning rubber reservoir that had shortly before been merely a simple nipple attached to the tip of my prick.

I tremble, right there on the spot, for a good five seconds, not sure where in the hell I am. My cock manages a couple complementary jerks, all its own, but it has already blasted all of my cum it's going to. These are merely its death tremors to tell me I'd better carefully pull it and its cum-filled rubber free of Niles' asshole before my cock softens to the point where its shrivelling makes it go AWOL from rubber and cum.

"Was that good for you, Niles?" My guts exploded, I'm not nearly as concerned for his well-being as I once was. No way do I have enough left in me to take him any farther, even if his climax is only a couple of cock pumps away. Still, it's the gentlemanly thing to ask, not to mention a good-for-business thing to express my sincere hope that he got all he's paid for.

"You're the best," he assures. "You're the very best."

I'm glad, because not even those compliments can get any more than I've already given. My dick is no longer the die-hard erection it once was.

My hands push between his ass and my crotch and find the open end of my rubber which miraculously still hugs the base of my dick. My fingers keep the rubber in place as I begin the slow pull of my cock and rubber from Niles' ass.

"Coming out," I say, although it can't be something he doesn't already know and feel.

Once all of my cock is removed from Niles' butt, I swear to God there's an audible "plop" when the cum-filled snout of my condom comes free, too. The ballooned latex looks downright pendulous where it droops from the head of my dick.

I try, albeit unsuccessfully, to keep my pubic hair free of the rubber when I try to get the condom actually completely turned loose of my dick.

Niles comes unbent, and its a miracle how neat and tidy he appears, still fully dressed, the hole in his trouser asscrack no longer visible. A quick couple of runs of his fingers through his hair puts all of those strands back into good shape. By comparison, my pants are still dropped around my ankles, my shirt still unbuttoned, my dick still slippery with the veneer of wet cum left behind by my finally removed rubber.

"I'd like that, please?" Niles says.

I think he means my cock. Maybe he figures it's good for seconds and already slicked for rubberless sloppy seconds. My dick still looks hard, but it's lost a good deal of its starch. It doesn't get back up an asshole as tight as Niles' asshole, even if I could ever be persuaded to fuck any such asshole with my unprotected prick.

"Please," he says and reaches for the condom whose loose end I've tied off. Maybe it's a growing concern for the environment, but a lot of guys pocket their used condoms, these days, rather than leave them scattered and leaking. It makes it far less slippery manoeuvring park paths after dark.

"You want my bag of used cum?" I'm still not sure I've this right.

"Unless you want it?"

I hand it over and don't bother to ask its intended use. Vaguely, I hope he's not involved in some kind of voodoo or black-magic cult who'll mix my sperm with chicken or human blood and call up unearthly demons. Certainly, he doesn't look the type. Then again, he doesn't look the type who'd covet my used condom, either.

Having what he wants, namely a fuck and the gift of my used condom, he leaves. Quick as that. One thing I like about this kind of fuck is that it doesn't require lengthy good-byes. You just get up, zip up, and get out. Which is pretty much what I do. Pausing only momentarily to wonder where Niles' cum went if he blasted his load. Is he walking around with the inside of his pants crotch slimed with the smeared slugs of his discharge? Is he one of those guys who climaxes but can't spurt cream? Does he make off with my condom full of pearly slime as some kind of substitute for his own?

Oh, the great mysteries of life. Their contemplation short-lived, believe me, in that neither Niles' spunk, nor the condom with my used cum, wherever either now is or isn't, is no longer any concern of mine.

I follow the route Niles has taken down the park pathway, although he's long since disappeared by the time I'm on my way.

I'm going to miss my nightly visits to Boyland Park. Fucking up a storm in the great out-of-doors is loads of fun and, once I started taking fees for my services, decidedly lucrative. I have more cash in my piggy bank, after this one summer's vacation, than I ever did the summer I worked for my Dad and my Dad's brother, Carl. I told my parents I wanted just this one summer to find a job on my own. I ended up saying I'd hired on with a jan-itorial service, because that seemed conveniently able to explain my keeping late hours. Dear Mom and Dad had been per-plexed, bemused, but finally had consented, as long as promised no such nonsense when the time finally comes for me officially to join in the family business and shoulder my fair share of family responsibilities.

Tonight, I have to be home early. Tonight, a lot of the park regulars have to be home early. Schools, all across town, start tomorrow. Boyland Park is the only park in the city, at least as far as I know, that caters to gay sex and, come the beginning of each school year, those kids who have too far to travel to reach the park, or those of us suddenly with too many school activities, and/or too much homework, often cut down considerably on our hours of whoring in the bushes.

I stop at a coffee shop, just outside the park perimeter.

Cort Forbes

During the summer, the place is usually always full, even this early in the evening. Tonight, though, there are only two other customers besides me. One is a butch young hustler I know by sight. He nods, one professional greeting another. The other guy is obviously a hobo fallen on hard times. He concentrates entirely on his careful-not-too-spill-a-drop sips from his cup, and he doesn't give me even a passing glance.

I finish my coffee and a sugar donut. Both the hustler and the bum still linger as I head on home.

Next day, though we've never met, nor seen each other before that first Gymnastics class, Vandermeer van Horne (who has just transferred in from Winthrop), and I know we're destined to get to know each other a helluva lot better.

Vandermeer sits off to one side by the side horse. I sit directly across the room from him, beneath the still rings. When the time comes where we're told to pair up for our training over the next few weeks, Vandermeer and I automatically circumvent all other comers and meet up in the middle of the tumbling mat.

He's not wearing a shirt and displays a chest thin but pleasantly compact. There's just the faintest trace of hair that runs the mere etch of his pectoral cleavage. Another trace of the same kind of almost invisible blond hair fans across the base of his lower belly. Beneath his gym shorts, his legs are equally blond-haired and golden-tanned.

I suspect more blond hair at his crotch and between the cheeks of his firm young ass, and that's later confirmed in the showers. My same shower-room glance at his nakedness shows me his uncircumcised cock so large as to be almost obscene.

His eyes are blue-green. When he smiles, which is often (but not always with sincerity), his left cheek splits attractively along a vertical axis. His teeth are white and even.

While he remains surprisingly aloof from the rest of our classmates, Vandermeer is always warm enough towards me, freely showing me his laughter and his smiles. He's always quick, too, to compliment when I manage a gymnastics manoeuvre correctly which, all bragging aside, is most of the time.

He and I touch often when spotting for each other on the various pieces of gymnastics equipment. It is an acceptable touching that's necessitated by the nature of the sport in which we're involved. Vandermeer's hands always press my sides to still my body as it hangs from the rings. His eyes always watch closely for mistakes in routines which can throw off my timing and balance — although such mistakes remain few and far between.

We never talk sex, beyond his passing mention of a girlfriend he's supposedly left at Winthrop but whom he still manages to bed on a regular basis.

There's something decidedly sexy about the way his hands sometime linger on my body for a second longer than absolutely necessary. My own hands are no less coy as they steady Vandermeer's chest, his waist, and/or his thighs for the various assigned routines. For weeks, we pretend our mutual caresses aren't preliminaries for sex.

It's a Wednesday when Vandermeer shows up on my doorstep. Gymnastics semi-finals are scheduled for the very next day. Semi-finals really nothing too difficult. For weeks our standard routines have been practiced on each piece of equipment. For semi-finals, everyone merely performs the same none-too-difficult moves, and we're graded against each other on a point system. In our class of twelve, the top four people will get an A.

"Hi," he says. He wears faded blue jeans, bulged at the

crotch. He wears dirty tennis shoes, a white T-shirt. "Thought I'd come by to see if you'd like to join me for a quick jog around the park."

"You want to jog around the park?" I estimate the distance. I'm really not all that much into physical exertion. I "do" sports only because it's what's expected. I'm in gymnastics, because it's "the" premiere sporting activity ever since our school has taken state three years running.

"Jogging will keep us in condition for tomorrow's semi-finals," Vandermeer says, as if we're horses training for the Kentucky Derby.

"It's not as if we're talking semi-finals for the Olympics," I remind him. "How about we just make it a walk?" His suggested destination is certainly ideal. Maybe we'll luck out and catch sight of a couple of guys going at it, hot and heavy, in the bushes. At which time, I can suggest to Vandermeer that he and I might try a bit of similar experimentation.

"It's easy for you, isn't it?" he interrupts my sensuous train of thought.

"What's easy?"

"Gymnastics."

"It's just a class I take for a PE requirement, isn't it?" I say. "That and the fact that varsity attracts some cool chicks." The latter, of course, is a bunch of bullshit. Not that's it's not true, but it is bullshit for him or me to think I'm supposedly interested in something so heterosexual as chick-attraction potential.

"Being first in class, then, doesn't mean all that much to you?" he says.

"First in gym class, you mean?" He's got to be kidding.

"Yeah."

"Well, I suppose I do want to make varsity but, as far as I see it, you're my only competition. The rest of our group hasn't the coordination of a drunk between them."

"What I'm saying is that winning is more important to me."

I've had that figured. Some people are geared to be competitive and go ape-shit if they don't always come out on top. Vandermeer doesn't come from a very wealthy family, and his whole future is tied up in his need to land big-money scholarships that require all sorts of A-one performances in the total school environment. On the other hand, my family has pretty much always had more than enough money, and I'll end up working for my father and my uncle in their real-estate business.

"You want to be top man in gym class, after semi-finals, I think that can be arranged," I tell him.

That's all it takes for his agreeing to let my cock fuck him. No need, any longer, to spot anyone sucking and fucking in the bushes of the park, from which I, then, derive an excuse to suggest Vandermeer and I try a little similar experimentation. Not even, any longer, any real need for me to come out and say, "Okay, I'm gay, so let's get naked and screw, even if you're straight as a stick!" That I will screw him no longer even needs verbalization, because it's mutually understood as an integral part of what he's just asked from me and what he's prepared to pay for it.

We find a secluded spot in the park. During the school week, there are always plenty available. We shuck every stitch of our clothes.

Vandermeer goes down on his back, bends his knees and fillets his legs in open invitation for me to drop down in between.

Within seconds, I've rubberized my cock and fucked it deep up Vandermeer's tight ass. His asshole reacts with a sensuously protesting ripple.

– 135 –

Cort Forbes

My balls cascade along the hard compact flesh of Vandermeer's upturned ass. My black pubic hair mingles with his blond, my muscled belly mates with his belly. Our nipples, one on one, chafe and harden.

I gently bite Vandermeer's left earlobe, and Vandermeer gasps. Whether it's a real gasp or expertly faked, I can't tell. What's more, by this stage, I don't much care.

Vandermeer kneads the flesh of my back and squeezes my asscheeks. His handholds on my butt tug my hips even closer into his saddle in order to bury my cock as deeply as possible up Vandermeer's rhythmically convulsing gut.

"Hard!" Vandermeer says. Obviously, he doesn't want me to come out of this feeling I've given up something for nothing. "Fuck me hard! Fuck me hard! Fuck me hard!"

I do my damnedest, sweat oozing from our bodies so that soft farting sounds occur wherever our damp flesh meets. My cock makes wet noises, too, as it distributes the lubricant fucked to Vandermeer's rectum by my rubber-sheathed erection.

Vandermeer lifts his legs and locks his ankles in the small of my back. He wraps his arms around my neck and pulls my face down hard against the hard muscle of his shoulder at his neck.

My compacting scrotum quickly has my nuts en route to the base of my butt-fucking erection. The muscles in my thighs tighten. The gymnastic-hardened muscles of my chest and arms bulge into attractive high-relief.

Between our mated bellies is his stiff and supine big cock. I grind his giant erection between us. If my hastily expanding pleasure precludes me from paying as much attention to his dick as I might have, had I come at this from an entirely different per- spective, I'm determined he won't entirely escape the pleasure. In that, I'm really not certain that he cares if he enjoys any of this or not. I'm really not certain that he isn't most concerned with his ability to use this as a necessary means to an end. However, if all of this is nothing to him but a well-orchestrated performance, likely only to happen again should similar circumstances arise, I take personal pride in trying my best to provide him with just a taste of the enjoyment to be found only in my arms and nowhere even to be hinted within the arms or cunt of his girlfriend.

I bite his neck, and Vandermeer's fingers clamp my neck and squeeze. He arches his neck, opens his mouth, and sighs rather than groans. His hand moves up the nape of my neck, his fingers suddenly in my hair. His parenthesizing legs tightened around my waist. His unsheathed cock oozes translucent dampness that pools in his indented navel.

He presses his full lips against mine. Our tongues collide, and Vandermeer's groan becomes one with one of my own. Our spit mingles and, though bland on our taste buds, is enough aphrodisiac to spur me into a hopefully longer, harder, faster fuck.

Our hips dance sensuously in tune to my cock's continued slipping and sliding within Vandermeer's butt. My dick swells larger. My cum-filled balls pulse with their increasing stockpile of pearly slime and, then, ache pleasantly as, once again, they're squashed against Vandermeer's upturned ass.

Sweat beads my forehead, drips into my eyes. My hair, wet with more sweat, plasters my thick dark hair strands against my scalp. My cheeks flush, my eyes shut. My throat hurts, and my breathing becomes more and more labored.

Vandermeer's breathing is equally as ragged as mine. His ribcage impressively swells and constricts to ride his swollen nipples persistently against the pinpricks erected on the circular brown nubs that punctuate my pectorals.

Every fiber of my body shudders beneath the intensity of my all-consuming orgasmic release. The muscles in my legs, my ass, my stomach, and my shoulders, bunch into even more impressive bas-relief. My balls, pulled so far up against the base of my dick that they seem lost within my lower belly, are held in place by my scrotum gone so prune-like, beneath the furring of my black pubic hair, as to appear downright bear-like.

My cum is great bolts of creamy goo that, finding nowhere else to go, pool within the welcoming rubber nipple that caps the head of my dick up Vandermeer's ass.

I open my mouth wide, and unsuccessfully I try coherently to verbalize the extent of those pleasures wracking my body.

"Now!" Vandermeer mutters beneath me, and I can't believe he's so late in his pronouncement of my orgasm which he surely must know has been going on for quite sometime.

I'm wrong, though, in assuming that he refers to my ejaculation. Maybe, all along, I've been way too insistent in seeing him merely as a heterosexual out to exchange homosexual favors for something he wants. He shows me a surprisingly more complex psyche by thrusting up his hips and simultaneously erupting great wads of his spurting cream to become quickly churned to butter beneath the intensely grinding dance of our mated bellies.

His hands grip frantically at the flesh of my back and shoulders, massaging my muscles violently as his wildly passionate groans echo in my ears.

My hips keep pumping, keep feeding him the last of my cream, as his cock empties all of his balls into what little remaining space exists between us.

In finale, I bang his ass so frantically with my lower belly that I actually bruise the flesh surrounding my cock at my balls.

The next day, Vandermeer is first in our gymnastics semi-finals.

I'm surprised the coach asks me to stay after.

Coach Wilkins joins me in his office and actually shuts the door behind us.

"You find gymnastics easy, don't you?" he says, although it's less a question than it might be.

"You're the second person, in as many days, who's said as much," I confess and wonder where this can possibly lead.

"I've watched you," he says. "You're always the first one done with any new routine. Do you ever think of asking me to show you something more complicated?"

"No." Any such notion that he even thinks I would is something that frankly surprises me.

"Would you mind telling me why not?"

"I don't get graded on anything other than the standard, assigned routines, right?"

"But you're obviously capable of more. What about the self-satisfaction of progressing to an advanced level before you're required to?"

"Come on, coach, I am, after all second, in the whole damned class."

"Who's first, I wonder?"

His question is rhetorical. He knows Vandermeer is first as much as everyone else, including I, know it.

"You and Vandermeer are good friends, aren't you?" he says instead.

"We spot for one another," I say and sound vaguely on the defensive. I am vaguely on the defensive.

"I'm not knocking your friendship," he verbally soothes my worried brow. "It's great. It's just that I don't think you, personally, should let it interfere with your class work."

"I don't understand." No way he knows what happened, between Vandermeer and me, in the park.

"What I'm telling you is as much for Vandermeer's benefit as it is for your own," he insists.

I wait for him to continue. I'm certainly not going to say anything to incriminate myself.

"Only two points separated you from Vandermeer in class standing today," he says. "Are you happy having lost out by so short a margin?"

"It's still an A, isn't it?" Anyway, it is unless he's changed his grading system without telling me.

"It's an A, " he confirms, then actually sighs. "Is that all that's important to you?"

I shrug.

"You gave a very sloppy side-horse dismount during semi-finals," he reminds. "Very sloppy. I don't think I've ever seen you give such a sloppy dismount, even during practice."

"I was nervous. This was semi-finals, not practice."

"You could have been top man in class if you hadn't conveniently muffed that one dismount," he accuses. "You could have been first if you'd tried only a little harder."

"So, I'll try harder next time." Although, he shouldn't hold his breath, waiting for that to happen. If I got my cock up Vandermeer's asshole when Vandermeer thought I could beat him at semi-finals, what can I achieve if Vandermeer ever suspects I'll wrench top honors from him during finals?

"If Vandermeer is really your friend, then you'll let him win first place only if he deserves first place," the coach says. "You won't hand it over to him on a silver platter because of some false sense of loyalty and friendship."

"You're not suggesting I threw the dismount on purpose?"

"Didn't you?"

"No!"

"Some people have to win to survive," the coach says. "Maybe you can't understand that, because you're the type of person to whom everything comes way too easily. Less naturally gifted people, less well-provided-for people, feel they have to be king of the mountain, every mountain. The sad part being, no one can ever be king of every mountain, every time. It's better for people to discover that while they're still young enough and flexible enough to make the necessary adjustments."

"Vandermeer is a good gymnast," I insist.

"Vandermeer is a very good gymnast," the coach agrees, "but he's not a natural. He works at it. The boy sweats blood. He comes in after-hours to work on his routines, while you're at home watching some video movie, attending some dance, getting to third base with some girl, or maybe just jacking off. How many times have you been up here on one of your free periods?"

"So?"

"You don't really have a clue, do you?" He sounds genuinely chagrined.

"Oh, I have a clue," I say, although I don't know what in the hell he expects from my understanding. If it's what I think, he's not only pissing off a bridge but into the wind. Gymnastics, after all, isn't one of my favorite subjects. Nor, although I'll probably excel in it, will it likely ever be.

"And?" Obviously, the coach wants some kind of commitment that I'm not at all prepared to make.

"And, what, coach? After all, who's going to look back in a few years and say that I got an A in gymnastics but was only second in my gymnastics class? No one. They'll just see an A if they bother to look at all."

"Would Vandermeer still be your friend if you'd won the semi-finals?"

But I hadn't won. What the point of what if?

Vandermeer had let me fuck his ass. I'd been top man in Boyland Park, even if he'd been top man in gymnastics class. To me, the first was far more important, not to mention pleasurable, than the second.

Besides which, the truth be known, Vandermeer had genuinely out-performed me on the side horse, even I having been taken back by just how good he'd been. Although, I'm not about to tell the coach that. Nor, for that matter, do I have any intentions of telling Vandermeer that, either.

I've other plans for Vandermeer.

THE END